SILAS

A Playboy's Lair NOVEL: PART ONE

S.R. WATSON

Silas (A Playboy's Lair Novel)- Part One
Copyright © 2017 S.R. Watson
First Edition: June 2017

ISBN-13: 978-1546969624
ISBN-10: 1546969624

Cover Design: Sommer Stein of Perfect Pear Creative Covers
www.ppccovers.com

Editor: Jenny Sims, www.editing4indies.com

Cover Model: Ryan "Stacks" Harmon
www.facebook.com/ryanstacksharmon

Photographer: Golden Czermak of Furious Fotog
www.onefuriousfotog.com

Formatter: Stacey Blake of Champagne Formats
www.ChampagneFormats.com

Other Books by S.R. Watson

Forbidden Trilogy
Forbidden Attraction (Available Now)
Forbidden Love (Available Now)
Unforbidden (January 2018)

Stand Alone
The Object of His Desire (Available Now)

S.I.N. Rock Star Trilogy
Sex in Numbers (Available Now)
Creed of Redemption (Available Now)
Leave it All Behind (Coming Fall 2017)

SILAS Music Playlist

In the Air Tonight - Natalie Taylor

Not Afraid Anymore - Halsey

Simple Things - Miguel

Nutshell - Alice in Chains

Insatiable - Prince

Halfway Right - Sarah Jaffe

Blindfold - Canopy Climbers

Tonight - Nonso Amadi

Black Flies - Ben Howard

Fantasy - Alina Baraz

Somebody to Love - Jasper Sawyer

Never be Like You - Flume

Bullet Train - Stephen Swartz feat. Joni Fatora

Underflow - Emma Louise

Everything - Lifehouse

Unsteady - X Ambassadors

The Heart Wants What It Wants - Selena Gomez

You Should Know Where I'm Coming From - Banks

To be Torn - Kyla La Grange

Tennessee Whiskey - Chris Stapleton

DEDICATION

I dedicate Silas to my amazing readers. Thank you for your continued support and enthusiasm for my novels. Your personal messages, social media posts, and feedback are inspiring and is greatly appreciated. You, my readers, are why I write. I love creating characters and worlds for you all to get lost in… creating sexy alphas for you to fall in love with. I love creating angst and mystery that keeps you on your toes in anticipation, before delivering the HEA. It's all about the journey so I'm glad that you all choose to take the journey with me.

A ship is always safe at shore, but that is not what it's built for.—Albert Einstein

PROLOGUE

Brennan

I T WAS JUST A FUCKING SWIM. A RASH DECISION that landed me in trouble with the Neumanns because I needed to feel close to her today. It has been twenty minutes since Mr. Neumann said we needed to talk. Everyone knows that the "we need to talk" spiel never pans out, so I'm probably about to get fired. A lone tear runs down my cheek as I look up at the clock on my wall. It's now a few minutes past six. Each tick makes me jumpier than the one before as my mind wanders back to the moment I was caught swimming laps in the pool a half an hour ago. I've always waited until I was sure that everyone was asleep. Midnight swims were my time to be free to think about her. Today, I didn't wait. The house was quiet, so I reasonably assumed that the Neumanns were out. They've never said that their pool was off-limits, but to be fair, I've never asked. Today marks the one-year anniversary of my mother's death. The day she took her own life. The day I found her in the bed next to me not breathing. I hate that I remember her this way—as the coward who left me alone. My daily swim helps me remember her before the ugliness. She taught me to swim when I was seven in the very pool I was caught in today. It was our thing. Each night when she was finished with all her work, we would sneak out to the pool for our mother-daughter time.

I didn't attend traditional school, so I didn't have a strict bedtime. I was usually in bed before eleven, but she never wanted to miss spending quality time with me because of her job. My homeschooling took place while Mom worked during the day. She'd set me up with my lessons for the day in the kitchen and the entire house staff checked on me in rotations throughout the day. They were all part of my learning. Thomas, the house manager, and Bertha, the cook, were my favorites. They would help make a game out of my lessons and created ways to help me remember what I'd learned.

A turn of my doorknob has me sitting straighter on my bed, halting my trip down memory lane. I pull the towel I'm still wearing closer around my body. I hadn't dared to move from this spot since I was sent here to wait. Thomas comes through the door, and my shoulders drop in relief. Even with all his responsibilities as the house manager, he's stepped up the most to make sure I was taken care of. He's the one who negotiated with the Neumanns for me to take over my mother's job after she died. They wanted someone with more experience, but he ensured them that I could handle it.

"Brennan, why haven't you changed into some dry clothes?" he asks in confusion.

"Well, because I didn't know when Mr. Neumann would be in here to talk to me. I didn't want to be in the middle of getting dressed when he came," I explain.

That's only partly true. It's mostly because I have been scared shitless of what he was coming to tell me and couldn't move from this spot.

"He's not coming, Bren. He sent me." The sadness reflected in his eyes confirms my prediction. He's sent Thomas in here to let me go, and the irony is not lost on me. The one person who I have come to trust the most will be the one to kick me out on my ass.

"Don't say it, Thomas. Please don't! I'll go." My stupid tears are really flowing now. I clench the towel tighter around me as if that could trap the wind that has just been knocked from my sails.

"I'm sorry. This is all Mrs. Neumann's idea. She didn't like that you were in the pool in a skimpy bathing suit. You're the only female left here, Bren, and she thinks you're a distraction," he says apologetically. "I don't agree with her assessment, but my hands are tied."

Mrs. Neumann is the one who found me in the pool, and she yelled at me to get out that instant. The smoldering disdain in her eyes was unprecedented. She stood there at the edge of the pool as I got out then threw me a towel big enough to get lost in. Her gaze held mine for the briefest of seconds before she turned on her heel and stormed off. That was it. No explanation or further chastisement. I waited until she had completely disappeared into the house before I escaped to my room, but Mr. Neumann was waiting for me as I passed the kitchen.

He stood near the sink with a grip so tight on the counter his knuckles were mottled white. His affect gave nothing away unlike Mrs. Neumann's. He simply stated that he needed to speak with me and would meet me in my room. Only he never came. He sent Thomas to get rid of me because his wife thought I was a *distraction*. It doesn't make sense. Yes, my one piece is a little on the small side. It's the last one my mother had bought for me before I developed these breasts that have taken over my body. I don't have much when it comes to clothes. Where in the heck would I wear them? I never venture away from the mansion, and I don't have friends bedsides my work family here. I wasn't trying to be a tramp or be inappropriate. If anything, I'm the complete opposite. I'm not a distraction, dammit. I don't want her husband or any of the men here. These people look out for me, and now, I'm being sent away from the only family I know.

"I found you another home," Thomas says, interrupting my thoughts.

"What do you mean found me another home? This is my home. No other place will be home," I rebut.

"Home, as in another place to work. With us is your real home," he clarifies. "I made a call to a long-time friend of mine who is also a house manager. His name is Mr. Davenport, and he was able to get you a job. I've shared this information with the Neumanns, and they've booked you a flight to Florida tomorrow morning."

I don't like this one bit. And across the globe, for Christ's sake. The idea of starting over somewhere else and meeting new people terrifies me. Hell, I've never even been on a plane. The Neumann's mansion has been my reality from birth. The older I got, the more I realized just how different my mom, the house staff, and I were. We didn't fit in with the privileged. When I turned twelve, my mother began to teach me how to clean and maintain a house—tools of the trade per se. From there, I learned other jobs such as cooking and gardening. My mother wanted me to be well rounded for when I found a husband because she didn't want this servant life for me forever. I remember thinking her reasoning was sexist and absurd, but I wanted to earn my keep, so I soaked up the knowledge anyway. It made me feel good to be able to lighten her workload with the skills she taught me.

Once, during my ninth grade year of high school, I tried to fit in the outside world, and I hated it. I only lasted a week in the "fancy private school for the rich" that Mr. Neumann got me into. To say I was an outcast would be an understatement. I never want to experience that feeling again—the not fitting in. I don't want to be the new girl again. But the truth is, I have no choice. I have some money that my mother left for me, and money that I've earned from my job with the

Neumanns, but I don't have the resources to get a place on my own just yet. I don't have any life skills or job skills aside from being a maid. This is my reality. I am the help.

"Fine. Thank you, Thomas. I'll pack my stuff. I still don't understand why I didn't get a warning. Why is it that after all the loyalty my mother gave to this place, they can be so quick to just get rid of me?"

Thomas has no explanations or answers to that riddle, and I know this isn't his fault. I restrain myself from asking more about this new job because it doesn't matter. I don't need details that I'll just be anxious over—more than I am already. He takes the hint that I want to be left alone when I turn my back to him. He apologizes one more time, pats me on the shoulder, and exits the room. I wipe my eyes with the side of my hands. They don't deserve my tears. I know this is more of Mrs. Neumann's decision than her husband's, but I don't care. I feel betrayed for my mother. She's gone—a year today—and nobody has even thought about that. Nobody questioned why I was in the pool to begin with even though taking an afternoon swim was so out of character for me. And now I will lose our special place—our special memory forever. That saddens me the most.

CHAPTER 1

Silas

THE START OF A NEW YEAR WHEN THE HOLIDAYS are over means it's time for the Lair men to meet and discuss our remaining cruises. I pour myself a glass of Macallan 64 from the decanter and soak up the sunshine while I wait for Kassius, Alistair, and Valentine to arrive. I head toward the reversed shaped bow of my yacht and stand overlooking the marina. I leisurely sip on the amber liquid of the refined scotch as I watch my guests begin to board on the second level. A line forms as security vets each person. Every other month, starting with January, my yacht either traverses the Atlantic or cruises to Caribbean destinations for a month. Each cruise has a theme, that is sexual in nature, for like-minded individuals. The Lair men host these coveted sexcapades. My waitlist is ridiculously long, and my selection criteria are calculatingly specific. Many have been on my waitlist since I introduced this unique experience three years ago. I have several sexually oriented businesses, but most are run by my chief executive officers. This yacht, *The Playboy's Lair*, is my primary domain when I'm not traveling to check on my other entities. It is by far the hardest to get an invite on, and I only entrust the proprietary make-up of the cruises to Kassius, Alistair, and Valentine.

The chuff of a helicopter interrupts my people watching. The guys are finally here. My t-shirt flaps against my chest from the wind vortex created from the chopper touching down on the helipad in front of me. My three cousins immediately get off, already discussing some woman they shared in an orgy last night. The details are muffled, at best, because of the noise from the helicopter, but they are supplying a pretty animated visual of the event. The three of them live in different states but met up in Chicago last night

for some fundraiser hosted by one of my uncles—
Alistair and Valentine's father.

"Sounds like you guys had a good time last night,"
I say once they're close enough to hear me over the
helicopter's slowing rotors. It will remain here until it's
time to take them back.

"Understatement, man. I may have to break my
one-night stand rule and look her up next time I visit
Chicago." Kassius elbows me for emphasis. He never
sleeps with the same woman more than once, so this
one must have had some magical unicorn pussy.

"I'd love to hear all about this miraculous woman,
but first, let's get down to business." The guys follow
me to the lounge area just outside my suite and pour
themselves a drink. Neither bats an eye at my exquisite
choice of liquor. Macallan is our drink of choice, and
the older, the better.

"So what do you have planned for this cruise?"
Kassius asks. The entire planning and execution of
this first cruise were solely handled by me. In previous
years, the themes have been handled by these guys. I
haven't been hands-on since the very first one. "Are
you doing the introduction to erotic spanking again?"

The guys know that I'm an ass man, and my kink
involves leaving my mark. The belt is my favorite, but
it depends on my partner and the sensation she can

most tolerate. The belt is for the more experienced. Last time, my focus was too narrow. I led a class for people to experiment with long-range tools, such as the belt, but a majority of them preferred to stick with short-range tools, such as the paddle—less impact.

"Something like that. You fuckers know me well," I chide. "I'm broadening it to impact play for the mostly experienced. I've accepted ten novice members, though, who have little or no experience with this type of play. I couldn't take on more than that because I don't want to be in teaching mode the entire cruise."

The premise of this cruise is that thirty guests (half men and half women) thoroughly versed in the world of impact play have been matched based on their profile and preference. Each man chosen has experience in both thuddy and stingy impact play to better offer variety for the woman they are paired with. Sting is high velocity, has a smaller impact area, and is felt on the surface area of the skin. Thud is more of a penetrating blow, has a wider impact area, and is felt deeper than the skin. I have selected ten guests (again half men and half women) who are complete novices to give them an opportunity to explore their curiosities and discover which realm of the spectrum of impact play they prefer.

I explain the focus of this cruise in depth before we move on to discuss their plans for the upcoming cruises. Valentine has decided to bring exhibitionism and voyerism together while Kassius will host an orgy. No surprise there. Alistair is still undecided and is playing with a few different themes. He will need to report to me with a final decision by the time I get back in a month. His cruise isn't until August, but we need ample time to select from the waitlist and give notice for invites. Any unavailability by those selected moves them to the bottom of the list. I don't hold spots. My guests pay handsomely for the privilege to be included on one of my cruises, so I don't play favorites.

The familiar sound of stilettos approaching causes the guys to pause midsentence in distraction. Only one woman has the key card capable of accessing my personal space, and that's Tory. I wasn't expecting her arrival until much later. She's part of my senior leadership team, but more importantly, my fuck buddy whenever I'm aboard. Busy with a new startup in Arizona, I haven't been on board for the last four months.

Her step slightly falters when she sees us all sitting here. She pulls at her fiery red tube dress that barely contains her tits. Her attempt to add a little more length to cover her ass nearly has them falling out. We watch in apt fascination. It's no secret that she's fucked us all. I may not make every cruise, but one of us is always on board. The only person her legs haven't spread for is Kassius, and that's because, up until now, he's been in a serious relationship. That same relationship is responsible for his aversion to anything more than a one-night stand. I know the feeling all too well. While I don't partake in that commitment shit, I don't see the harm of keeping a casual fuck around if she serves a purpose. I outline my expectations and what I'm willing to offer ahead of time, and those who oppose get the boot.

Tory started as a housekeeper on my staff two short years ago. She made it very apparent that she was willing to serve more than just my cleaning needs. I've never mixed business with pleasure until her—my only exception. Her contributory fuck keeps us from being tempted to play with our guests. She ensures we're well satisfied for the month we're out at sea.

She slows her stride even more as she gets closer, unsure if we've discussed our time with her. She runs a nervous hand through her silky blond hair, attempting to tame the flyaways.

"Sorry, Silas. I wasn't aware you had company. I can come back later," she offers.

"Oh, we're company now?" Alistair speaks up. The other two look just as amused. Kassius leans back against the chair and crosses a muscled leg over his knee. Her eyes follow before darting back among us, unsure.

"Why the formality, my dear Tory? Every single one of us has been ball's deep in you with the exception of Kassius here." I pat him on the chest for good measure.

"No fret, sexiness. Sharing is what we're into, so you're in luck. You have nothing to fear or be ashamed of. Your pussy is an exquisite unicorn that we all enjoy," Valentine assures.

She is not at ease, and I know why. She is waiting for me to weigh in—for my approval. I wink in her direction and give her my genuine "I don't give a rat's ass" smile. She's not mine. I don't do mine. She visibly relaxes as she pushes those fake tits out in pseudo confidence. Kassius perks up at the gesture. He loves tits.

"Don't just stand there. Come have a seat," he suggests.

I can see the wheels turning in that mind of his. His devious thoughts are paper thin. We all give each other the look because we know where this is heading. When Tory attempts to sit beside him, he pulls her onto his lap. She doesn't stop him. Kassius slides a dubious hand inside her dress to cup one of her breasts, looking for any indication that she doesn't want this. She licks her lips in anticipation, and that's all it takes. He slides her dress down to her waist and catches a taut pink nipple between his teeth. I sip on my Macallan, happy to look on. A low moan slips from her pursed red lips as he buries his other hand between her legs. Valentine gets up and joins me on my side of the sofa. He refills his glass and settles in for the show. Apparently, he's sitting this one out too.

Alistair isn't sitting out, though. He stands and frees his cock before joining the scene. Kassius extends him the invitation to join by first lifting Tory enough to slip on a condom. He then wastes no time impaling her on his shaft while Alistair inserts himself in that skillful mouth of hers.

Moans and the slapping of flesh pierce the air in a hedonistic flair. My own cock stiffens to a semi from the sight and sounds. I don't play well with others, though. I'm a selfish son of a bitch. The guys know this about me because they've tried to get me to join their orgies before. Besides that, I'm into some way kinkier shit, and I prefer to explore with her later, once they're done having their fun.

I know my reasons for sitting out, but Valentine's

reason is unclear. "Had too much fun last night, fam? That mystical cunt gotten to you?" I nudge him, and he laughs.

"Impossible, fucker. No, I have plans tonight once we leave here. It's going to be a long night, so I'm giving my dick a break. That, and sometimes I just like to watch."

This from the guy hosting the exhibitionist-voyerism cruise. Again, no surprise there. That's his kink. He likes to watch and be watched. No more words between us as we watch Alistair and Kassius bend Tory like a pretzel. They leave no hole unexplored, stuffing her full of their cocks. Her face flushes in an orgasmic glow as she takes everything they offer her. Every stroke has her cries of passion reaching new heights until she's literally stuttering out the word fuck. They've worked her into a position of double penetration now as all three chase their impending orgasm.

Tory's legs begin to tremble just before she falls over the edge. I knew she would be first. Neither man would allow themselves to come until she did. It's in our guy code. Kassius and Alistair piston their hips in effortless synchrony until they both give in to the nut that was waiting to explode. They ease out of her slowly, and I feel like I should applaud that performance. They help her to her feet as she tries to make sense of the dress that is still coiled around her waist. I should have known she wasn't wearing panties underneath. She's sort of a freak like that. They escort her off—to shower together, I'm sure. That's their other MO. That way they can get her to suck them off for round two. In return, they will get her off with their fingers. Once the condom comes off, no more dick is involved. I know my cousins well.

"I guess our meeting is adjourned; wouldn't you say, cousin?" Valentine has always had a penchant for stating the obvious.

"I would say so. I would offer for you guys to stay for dinner, but as you've already stated, you have plans."

We hold these meetings as more of a formality than a necessity to make sure we're on the same page. Often, they also give us some time to catch up. Pussy has shortened this trip, but I'm confident we're on track. I'll get my tech guy the client list based on what we managed to discuss. Using his patented algorithm, he'll match the guests from the waiting list per our criteria and their preferences for our upcoming cruises. I'm planning to ask Kassius to hang back for a bit longer than the other two. He is the perfect suitor for what I have in mind—for the task I omitted discussing during our brief meeting.

CHAPTER 2

Brennan

THIS MUST BE SOME SORT OF MISTAKE. I SLOW blink a few times to clear the illusion in front of me as the limo I'm in pulls into an entrance that says Bahia Mar Marina. There are just so many boats … little ones and ginormous ones. We continue through the parking lot until only the ships are left. These are the biggest of them all. That's it. I'm dreaming. I'm still asleep on the plane, heading toward Fort Lauderdale. That is the only explanation for why I'm staring at all these ships in front of me.

Then realization creeps through like a wrecking ball, threatening to unravel my sanity. I'm going to be working on one of these monstrosities. A fucking ship! When Thomas said I was being transferred to work somewhere else, he didn't say anything about working on a ship. What kind of fuckery is this? Now, I regret not pushing for more details about this new job. Who is going to clean that floating city? I still want to hold on to the dream theory, or that maybe we're just picking someone up from here. This can't be my final destination.

My illusion bursts as the driver gets out and unloads my things from the trunk. I only have three suitcases. The wobbly wheels and worn fabric are at odds with the luxury surrounding us. The poor driver—Adam, I think he said his name was—has probably never had to handle such beat-up luggage. To me, it still zips and still rolls, so it's good enough. Everything I've ever owned has been secondhand. I try not to focus on the unfairness of it all. Now, judging by all these ships, it seems I'm going to work for someone who has even more money they don't know what to do with. Why in the hell else would someone buy a ship this pretentious? These aren't like the regular boats we passed on the way in—these are another level of rich. I don't know much about boats, but when I was younger and naïve, I foolishly let myself dream about one day being able to get on a ship just like these. In the magazines left in the Neumann's parlor, I'd see people smiling and sipping champagne on ships like these. I used to sneak some of the magazines back to my room and spend hours studying the lifestyles of the rich and famous. I wanted their life. One week in a private school in Los Angeles cured me of such childish fantasies, though. I learned real quick that I wasn't their equal and could never hope to be. Those who had the money held the power. I learned my place—bitterly so, but still a lesson all the same.

An older silver-haired gentleman dressed in khakis and a button-down shirt meets us at the limo. He introduces himself as Atticus to the driver and explains he is here to take me on board. He turns to me and greets me with a warm smile. The vibe I get from him puts me at instant ease for some reason, which is rare. He stretches his hand out for me to shake, and I take it.

"Hi, there. You must be Brennan. Thomas has told me so much about you," he says as he grips my hand firmly. Funny because Thomas left much information to be desired about my new "home" that's not even a home. It's a damn ship. "My name is Mr. Davenport, but you can call me Atticus. I'm Mr. Lair's house manager, so to speak, but on a boat. I see to all the affairs related to his staff and oversee daily operations."

"Nice to meet you, Mr. Dav—I mean Atticus," I correct myself. "I want to start by being honest," I offer. Atticus arches one of his silver eyebrows at me in question. "Sure. Honesty is always the best way to go," he assures.

"Well, when Thomas told me he got me another job similar to the one I had, he didn't exactly tell me it was on a ship. At the Neumann's estate, I was only responsible for cleaning a fraction the house. I don't have any experience cleaning ships," I explain, pointing at the colossal boats surrounding us.

"I'm sure I won't be the only maid working for Mr. Lair, but I just want to be upfront about my experience."

Atticus chuckles a bit but quickly schools his expression.

"I'm glad you were honest with me, Brennan. It speaks volumes about your integrity. The ship you're referring to is called a yacht—a mega yacht. It's a type of ship, though, since it's four hundred feet long. With that being said, Mr. Lair doesn't employ maids. I don't much like the term myself. Seems derogatory. We prefer the term housekeeper."

He pats me on the shoulder, and his heartwarming smile is back in place. I'm glad I got that out even though I probably seem like a dummy for not knowing these boats were all yachts. Then again, that distinction is more familiar to the people who can actually afford to buy one. Or in Atticus's case, having worked aboard one.

"You will get the training you need, but be assured that the staff aboard *The Playboy's Lair* is plentiful," he continues. "We have a crew of fifty-eight."

For the first time, I see the name *The Playboy's Lair* italicized on the side of one of the yachts at the end of a wooden dock. Mr. Lair's "yacht" is called *The Playboy's Lair?* What kind of boat is this? A better question would be what goes down on this boat? What has Thomas gotten me into? Is this why he was so nonchalant about the specifics of this job—why he didn't offer any extra info? An onslaught of new questions rush me, and my legs grow weak. I was safe where I was. I hate the unknown. I hate meeting new people, waiting for them to judge me. *Ugh.*

"Shall we?" Atticus asks after grabbing two of my suitcases from the driver. I grab the remaining suitcase in a death grip. I nod, but the flood of butterflies in my belly is screaming hell no.

"Is this everything?"

"Yes, I don't have much." He smiles in understanding and nudges me forward to walk down the dock.

The three large suitcases had belonged to my mother. I stuffed two of them with as much of her stuff that I could. I needed to bring her with me since I would no longer have the pool we spent time in. That was a big part of my memory of her that I left behind. I'm grateful I was able to find her sacred shoebox full of the pictures she took before I left. The old shoebox even had an old Olympus camera she used and a few rolls of undeveloped film. I looked through it all but didn't find a single picture of my father. She had a plethora of pictures of different flowers in bloom and statues from around the mansion as well as a lot of candid shots of me from when I wasn't paying attention. Sadly, not many pics of her were in that box either.

At some point, I bump into Atticus, who is walking beside me. Allowing my mind to drift back to better times momentarily warded off my sense of dread. Now each step feels laced with lead.

"I know all this can seem overwhelming, Miss, but try not to worry," Atticus says like he's reading my mind. "Mr. Lair is really a great employer to work for. I have been with the Lair family for forty years."

Something about him puts me at ease when he talks, like when he introduced himself. He reminds of Thomas in a way—nurturing. Maybe the name of the yacht is an inside joke or a tribute to Mr. Lair's older playboy days. It could simply be just a name and not an indication of the type of boat it is—like that of the Playboy Mansion of Hugh Hefner. *That's it.* I'm jumping to conclusions. Atticus seems like a sweet grandfatherly type. Not the type to work on some sex ship ... yacht ... whatever the hell it is.

"That's comforting to hear," I reply genuinely. We finally enter the massive "floating mansion," and I'm taken aback by its opulence. It's absolutely beautiful. It looks like we've stepped onto some futuristic spaceship. Gold speckled, black marble stairs wind down from above in the shape of an intricate snail. Hanging chandlers pick up the shimmering lights from the water just below the staircase. Unique looking golden furniture pieces add cohesion to the space. I've never seen anything like this in any of the magazines, and I've studied more than I can count. I don't have to have ever stepped a foot on a boat to know this décor is not typical. *The Playboy's Lair* is by far the biggest and flashiest yacht here in the marina, so it makes sense that the interior would be nothing less.

Atticus gives me a few minutes to look around before redirecting me to a set of gold elevators behind us. He places a black key card in a slot near the illuminated numbers before pressing the number three. It's the last floor before the one marked TPL. I'm guessing that stands for The Playboy's Lair.

"Is this the floor where I'll be staying?" I ask as the elevator dings on the third floor.

"No. You'll be staying on the first floor. Staff stays on either the first or second floor of the forward of the boat. This floor has the meeting room, a lounge, an indoor pool, and the dining area. A few suites are located on this floor, but they are for the senior leadership staff. You're the only new hire among us, so I'll go over the layout of the floors, your assignment, uniform, area restrictions, and most importantly—the nondisclosure agreement."

That last bit piques my interests. Area restrictions? Nondisclosure agreement? The sinking feeling that this is more than I bargained for returns with a vengeance.

"You'll meet most of the staff tomorrow. As they arrive, they have separate preparations to complete before we cast off. Some are already on board, but they're situating the incoming guests. We cast off in a little over an hour."

"And go where?"

Of course, it's a boat. I didn't even think of it actually going anywhere. It's all starting to seem fishy, pun intended. Thomas had me apply for a passport long before the pool incident. Did he know the Neumanns were looking to get rid of me? He said that having a passport was better than just the regular ID that I had. I trusted him. What was he keeping from me?

"I will explain everything, but first I have to explain some expectations and have you sign an NDA." After a brief pause, he shares a little tidbit more to pacify me. "We're heading to St. Maarten first with stops at several Caribbean ports to follow. We will return in a month."

Okay, that tidbit somewhat distracts me from my conspiracy ideation. I've never been out of Los Angeles before now, let alone the country. This would have been a wonderful experience for my mother. I can only imagine all the pictures she could have taken. Then again, if she was still alive, we'd still be at the Neumanns. They probably just kept me around for an acceptable amount of time after her death in an effort not to appear harsh. I can't help the animosity I feel toward them now. They made Thomas tell me they were letting me go on the anniversary of her death. I try not to think about that sad fact. I have a chance to see the world, and I know just how I can pay patronage to my mother's memory. First, I need to get my hands on a new camera—one of those digital ones.

"This way," Atticus says, leading me into a room with a large table in the center.

More gold decorates this room with black and

white marbled floors. The chairs are white with golden legs to bring the continued color scheme full circle. Mini screens peek from the confines of the long oval table. High tech yet sophisticated. I notice the manila folder at the head of the table as Atticus pulls out a chair for me. I take a seat and pull it closer. My name is scrawled across the top in bold black letters. Atticus takes a seat beside me and takes the folder from me. He grabs a document out of the folder before handing it back to me. Suddenly, an air of business has made us more formal. No heartwarming smile to ease the seriousness of this moment.

"I'll summarize the contents of the agreement while highlighting the most crucial aspects in favor of time," he says, waving the document he just took from the folder. "Stop me if you don't understand or have questions about something. It's very important that you know what you're signing. You will not get a copy. It's confidential and must remain in Mr. Lair's possession."

It's gone as quick as it appears, but I see it. *Weariness.* Whatever the cause of it, I'm embarking on foreign territory.

Atticus discusses the NDA. He explains that there is no need to venture further if I don't sign. He rips the Band-Aid off my naïvety without warning. This is a *SEX* boat! Two floors in the aft are not accessible to staff unless they're designated to work those floors. My duties will be limited to the middle part of the boat, called the amidship, and is where the guests of the *Lair* mainly interact. The restricted first and second floor of the aft is accessible by two different colored key cards. Atticus doesn't go into specifics about what is on each floor, only that it's adult … i.e. sexually related. Guests take this cruise to experience whatever kink they paid for. They can't visit both restricted floors; they can only visit the one they signed up for, hence the different colored key cards.

The kinky crap stays in the back of the boat, so that's refreshing. But everywhere else is considered neutral territory, which includes two cinemas, multiple lounges and bars, gyms, an indoor pool, an outdoor pool, and some other amenities I can't remember. Atticus listed them but no need to retain them all since employees only have access to the amenities in the forward part of the boat. The indoor pool is located on the third floor forward, so that's a win for me. The forty guest suites are situated on the first and third floor midship. I mentally keep track of all the information being thrown at me and summarize that the first and second floor in the aft is for kink, mid is neutral space and guest rooms, forward is for the staff, and Mr. Lair occupies the top floor.

I'm not sure I want to know what goes on in the back, but as long as that's where it stays, I'll be fine. Rich people are so weird. I'm assured no legality worries exist, but the NDA bounds me from discussing any aspects regarding Mr. Lair's business operations or any guests who have been aboard. Atticus reassures me ample security will protect me against guests if needed. It is against the rules for us to have any inappropriate interaction with them. Invitations are only sent to a select forty people per cruise to maintain an intimate, prestigious experience. According to Atticus, many have been on *The Playboy's Lair* waiting list for years. Only the most elite even know about the cruise. The Neumann's had house parties with guest lists in the hundreds, and I managed, so I can do this for a chance of a lifetime to travel the world. That, and let's face it, I'll be out on my ass if I don't.

"Okay," I say after Atticus finally pauses and looks at me. His eyebrows knit together.

"Okay?" he repeats.

"Where do I sign?" I ask, reaching for the agreement.

"Just be sure, Brennan. Don't take any of this lightly. This is not ..." He doesn't finish his sentence. Instead, he places the document in front of me and hands me the pen from his shirt pocket. He waits patiently as I sign my name next to the x. This is it. I've sealed my fate.

Atticus takes the NDA from me but lets me keep the manila folder. "I'll show you to your cabin so you can get settled. I've decided that I don't really need to go over the rest of the contents of the folder. It's just new hire stuff, and I know you can read. It'll give you all the info you need about your shift, duties, uniform, etc. You will be buddied with Tory to start your training tomorrow. She's our senior housekeeper and will help you get acclimated. She'll size you for a uniform tomorrow morning before you start." We walk in silence until we reach my cabin on the first floor.

"A woman by the name of Glenda was supposed to be your roommate, but she had a death in the family and won't make this cruise. Normally, staff without seniority have a roommate. We're aren't going to change room assignments this late, though, so it looks like you'll get a cabin to yourself." Atticus chuckles. *Friendly Atticus is back.*

"I know you hired me as a favor to Thomas, but thank you for the opportunity," I say.

Even though this job is not what I would have pictured for myself, I have a job because of him. He reaches for my hand again to shake, and I spontaneously go in for a hug. He stiffens initially before settling into my embrace. I don't know what came over me—nostalgia maybe? I'm feeling ambiguous. On the one hand, I left the one place that contained all the memories of my mom and me, and it's hard to say goodbye to that. On the other hand, though, I have a chance for a new journey. One that I think my mom would be happy to see me take, even with the kinky people involved. I get to see and hopefully do things that she never got a chance to experience. I get to have a small piece of the lifestyle afforded only to the rich. Not the pretentious part, but the part that lets me broaden my horizons.

CHAPTER 3

Brennan

THE ALARM BLARES LIKE A SIREN IN THE SMALL confines of my cabin. I get tangled in the blankets trying to reach it to turn off the offending noise. Gah, I'm sure they can hear the stupid thing in the next cabin over. I finally break free, but the room is still dark since the curtains are closed. I feel around the bedside table until I have the clock in my grasp and then for a few more seconds until I find the snooze button. Okay, that was annoying. I don't want to be traumatized every morning by that thing. Last night, I purposely set it a couple of hours earlier than I'm scheduled to meet with this Tory person. I want to see the indoor pool we can use on the third floor, but I also want to watch the sun rise.

I push the blankets back and make my way to the light switch near the door. I forgot there was an electronic button by the bedside table to operate the lights and the curtains. Oh well, I had to get up anyway. The room is bathed in light, which reflects off all the cherry wood furniture in the room. It's so pretty. I love my new space. It's better than my room at the Neumann's, hands down. No expense was spared on décor or comfort. The mattress and bedding alone feel like they were made for a princess. I slept like a baby after I decided to have dinner in my room last night—well, until that alarm clock ruined my slumber. I didn't even get a chance to try out the fancy flat-screen TV mounted on the wall, but I'll remedy that tonight. Aside from the pool, I have everything I need right in here.

For now, though, I need to get a move on if I want to check out this pool. I quickly throw my midnight black, waist-length hair into the bun I usually wear. The mere thickness of it is too much of a hassle to do anything else with it. I've contemplated just cutting it all off, but I chicken out every time. The bun is not very stylish, but it's convenient. If I cut it, I may have to actually style it. I throw on a hooded long-sleeve shirt and sweatpants. I'll shower and get dressed for work after I get back. It's nearly 6:15, so I need to hurry.

It's only a couple of flights up, so I don't bother with the elevator. I haven't walked far before the indoor pool comes into sight. The water sloshes against the sides with each sway of the boat. The ocean must be rough this morning. The curtains are already pulled back to give a panoramic view through the floor-to-ceiling windows that look through to a spa of some sort.

It's not as deep as the Neumann's twelve-foot pool, but I can definitely swim laps with the eight feet of this one. I'll have to find out what time is acceptable to avoid another fiasco. I follow the winding staircase off to the right that leads to yet another level. Surprisingly, this level is open to the outside where you can walk out to the railing of the boat and look out at the ocean. The waves and the salty smell in the air are very soothing. I watch as the sun peeks from behind the clouds, bringing with it an array of yellow and orange hues. It's synonymous with my new start.

"Enjoying the view?" a male voice asks from behind me. Startled, I spin around on my heels, and the vision in front of me causes my breath to catch.

A gorgeous man stands before me, not even two feet away. His piercing blue eyes hold me captive, and I can't look away. Definitely no man who looked like him existed back at the mansion. Aside from his striking, gorgeous eyes, his brown with a hint of sun kissed hair is absolutely yankable. Shorter on the sides with considerable length on top for a woman to hold on to—just rolled out of bed tousled hair looks good on him. His mustache and beard contain just the right amount of facial hair without being too much.

"I'll take that as a yes. Seems like you are enjoying the view very much," he continues with a smirk. His dimples and perfect kiss-worthy lips add to this visual indulgence until he opens his mouth.

And just like that, the trance is broken. *Smug fucker.* He's obviously talking about himself now because I'm sure I look like a staring idiot. It's not my fault I have minimal exposure to hot guys—like none!

"Well, I was enjoying the ocean view and sunrise until I was interrupted," I lie. The truth is, I was enjoying both views—him and the other stuff I mentioned—until he opened that conceited trap of his. "Do you work here?" I need to get the subject off his handsomely good looks.

Mr. Smug raises his perfect eyebrows at me in amusement. "What do you mean?"

"You know? The thing people do to earn money—work? It's also known as a job. Do you work on this boat?"

Although I can't picture Mr. Smug Hottie being part of the help, I secretly hope so. Otherwise, it means he's a guest and off-limits. Who am I kidding? I could never pull a guy like him anyway, but it doesn't stop my vagina from reacting to this manly specimen. She perked up the minute his eyes met mine.

He seems to be a bit self-absorbed, so it cancels out his handsome sex appeal. I'll just keep telling myself that.

"No. I don't work on this boat then." Mr. Smug Hottie grins. "What about you? Do you work on this boat?"

"Yes. I'm the new maid … um, housekeeper. Today is my first day, but I'm pretty sure you're not supposed to be out here."

"Why is that?" He steps closer, and my breath hitches for the second time. I stupidly look into those blue eyes again, and I'm rendered speechless. When I'm finally able to string together a coherent sentence, I stutter like a babbling idiot.

"This area, the … the … the forward of the boat is for the … the … employees. The guests have their own pool," I finally get out.

"Ah, too bad. I happen to like this one," he taunts. "I guess that makes me a rebel. Although, technically, the pool is down there," he says, pointing at the pool one level below. *He's got me there.*

"Look. I'm not going to snitch on you, but you can't be on the forward of the ship. Guests are only supposed to be on the midship or aft. I don't want to be caught with you out here. I need this job," I almost plead. He's right about the pool thing, but this area is still off-limits.

"Yeah, that wouldn't be good. After all, snitches get stitches." He lets out the most infectious laugh I've ever heard, and those dimples are so damn enthralling. I want to yell at him because he is not taking me seriously, but I can't. I try to hold it in, and then I finally crack.

"Who in the hell even says that?" I giggle.

"Please don't tell me you've never heard that saying?" he teases. "It's street slang. A reference about not snitching to the cops?"

"Well, surprise, I wasn't raised in the streets."

I take a really good look at him now. He's wearing joggers and a t-shirt that clings to his chiseled chest and abs. He runs a hand through his already tousled hair, and my eyes follow. I cross one leg over the other to encourage my vagina to settle down. He looks down

at my crossed legs momentarily before his sinful lips
curve upward. Does he realize the effect he is having
on me? I give him another once-over, perusing the
god-like body his attire is doing so little to hide. Only
sexual perfection, nothing that screams he was raised
in the streets either.

"And from the looks of it, you weren't either," I add
sarcastically, hoping he doesn't see through my lustful
thoughts.

"Ah, but you don't have to be raised in the streets
to have street smarts." He winks at me, and I swear my
stupid vagina winks her approval. "It was nice talking
to you, Miss. I'll get going before you're seen with
me. Wouldn't want you to get in any trouble on my
account."

That sexy grin is back. It hints at an underlying
meaning, and I wish I knew what. He probably knows
that he'll make an appearance in my next get myself off
session.

"Hey! Quick question before you go," I rush out
like I wasn't just mentally cataloging him for later. He
turns back slowly to face me, and I have to force myself
to continue. It's not fair for one man to be this sexy.
Now his stride toward me is turning me into mush.
"Um, where can I get a camera? Do you know if there
is a shop to buy that sort of thing on this boat?"

31

"There is a small gift shop amidship, but I don't think you'll find a camera in there. What kind were you looking for?" he asks.

"Just a digital one. One that doesn't need film." He bellows out a laugh; only this time, it's not so funny. He tapers it off after he realizes I'm serious.

"I'm sorry. It's just that ...Well, do those film based cameras even still exist? Unless you need one of those fancy cameras for something specific, why can't you just use the camera on your phone? Most phones nowadays come with decent megapixels. What kind of phone do you have?"

The pregnant pause between us is awkward. "I don't have one," I finally admit.

"What happened to it?" he pushes.

"I've never owned one." More silence. "I've never needed one." He shakes his head as if to clear it.

"Well, I'd better get going. Maybe you can get one at our first stop. Hopefully, you'll find one," he says. "It was nice meeting you ... I don't even know your name. What is it?"

"Brennan," I reply simply.

"Hmmm. That's a guy's name, but it somehow fits you. Take care, Brennan. I'm sure we'll see each other again real soon."

"Wait. You didn't tell me your name," I blurt out,

stopping him for the second time.

"You're right. Where are my manners? My name is Silas." He winks. I guess that is his signature move to make the panties wet because he definitely has it mastered. "Can I share an observation with you, Brennan?"

"Shoot," I encourage.

"I think you secretly want to get caught out here with me." With that bomb, he turns and walks away, chuckling to himself.

He stirs so much in me. So much so that I'm surprised by my body's reaction to him. I don't know what he meant about seeing me again real soon, but I'd be lying if I said I wasn't looking forward to it. So what if he's off-limits? I couldn't have him anyway. Whatever, it doesn't hurt to look and maybe get off to thoughts of him. I wonder what kind of kinky experience he's here for. Chances are, he is already here with someone. Anyway, the moment is over. I stayed out here longer than I'd anticipated talking to the handsome, smug stranger. Now I have to forgo a shower in order to meet with Tory on time.

There is an unexpected knock on my door. I give myself one more look over in the mirror before I open it. A blonde bombshell stands before me wearing a black pants suit that hugs her every curve. The buttons on her white button-down shirt strain against her bosom. It is obviously part of a uniform since the breast pocket of the jacket is embroidered with The Playboy's Lair logo. The blonde looks me up and down, and I can see the silent judgment in her narrowing eyes. I'm wearing a suit too; only mine is a mustard-colored skirt combination and about two sizes too big. It was my mother's.

"Hi. I'm Tory. You'll be shadowing me for your initial training today. I've come to get you fitted for your uniform before we go topside, and it would appear I'm here not a moment too soon." I bite my tongue at her obvious insult. So she's Tory? She doesn't look like any housekeeper I've ever seen.

"Can I come in?" she asks when I don't respond right away.

"Sure," I say, stepping aside. She wheels in a rack of uniforms. They are all collared, button-down gray shirts and black pants. The shirts bear the same logo as her jacket, but nothing remotely close to the sexy sophistication she's wearing.

"What size are you?" she asks. There is no friendliness in her tone.

"I'm a size six." I keep my tone just as dry. The employees didn't have to wear uniforms at the Neumann's unless they were frontline employees, meaning they were going to be in proximity with their guests—basically for entertaining purposes.

"Hmmm. We have a few size fours and a couple of eights. No way you could squeeze into a four, though." She winces while looking at my backside. My ass isn't exactly small and perky.

"I'm a size four, I mean," she adds as if that justifies her below the belt insult. "We'll put you in the eight. With a belt, you'll be fine. I'll fit you with a large shirt to make sure it fits over the girls," she says, pointing at my more than a handful boobs.

"Okay."

Suddenly, my optimism is sucked right out of me. I'm the outsider—the new girl. To make matters worse, I have Barbie here making me self-conscious about my considerable assets. We all can't have long legs, a lithe, tight body, and huge boobs. Well, I have the boobs part, but I'd kill for her proportions. She's every man's fantasy. She's the kind of woman who Mr. Smug Hottie would notice.

Will all the staff be this condescending? Will they all have the "just stepped off the runway" good looks like she does? Maybe Mr. Lair only employs gorgeous people like Tory for his sex ship, and I'm the anomaly—the favor. I enter the bathroom to put on the uniform while she waits. Just as I thought, it hangs on me without any type of shape. Not a curve to be seen. Not that I could hold a candle to her body. But it doesn't matter; this is how most of my clothes fit anyway since I wear a lot of my mother's things. I blow out a much-needed breath and rejoin Tory.

"Perfect," she exclaims. "It's a little big, but once you start cleaning, you'll appreciate the extra breathing room."

"How do you clean in that?" I foolishly ask. She's wearing hot pink "fuck me" stilettos, for God's sake. They're a far cry from the slip-resistant clogs that were issued to me last night.

"Oh, honey, I don't clean anymore. I supervise. Those days are behind me." She flips her bottled blond locks for added emphasis. "We have to get going. There's been a slight change to our schedule. Mr. Lair has called an impromptu meeting on some changes we need to know about."

I look at my naked face once more in the mirror and make sure my bun is securely bobby pinned in place. Standing next to Tory is giving me a complex, and I've never been one to care about makeup and crappy glamour girl stuff.

"I'm ready," I lie effortlessly. My feelings have been all over the place since I got here. Bosom Barbie sure as hell isn't making things any better. I wish Atticus was training me. Wonder if he'll be at this meeting?

I walk into the same conference room where I signed the NDA yesterday. The room is filled with people wearing uniforms similar to mine with slight style variations. Aside from Tory, they all seem like regular working people—not a single glamour bot in the bunch. I can feel their stares on me as I stand and wait for Tory to finish her conversation with the wiry, short-haired woman who has stopped us. She doesn't seem too pleased with Tory's response to her issue is all I can really piece together. They're in deep discussion about it, but I try not to eavesdrop. A quick scan around the room when we first walked in gives me an idea of who I'll be working with. It looks like mostly an older crowd, so that's a plus. If I had to guess, I'd say their ages range from late thirties to maybe early sixties, which is the same demographic I'm used to working with. Tory must have been the youngest before I arrived. I would guess her to be mid-twenties. I'm just glad she is the outlier. I don't think I could work with a bunch of people who looked and acted like her.

"Oh, you don't have to wait on me, Brennan. I'll catch up with you after the meeting," Tory says when she notices me still standing there.

A fake smile is plastered on her overly made-up face, but I'm not fooled. Not sure what her deal is, but whatever. I don't even bother to acknowledge her dismissal. Instead, I look around the room to find an available seat. A couple of seats are available closest to the entrance, but it's at the head of the table. I'm guessing Mr. Lair may take one of those seats when he arrives, and I don't want to be in the front.

I make my way to the back of the room to take the last available seat before someone snags it. The voices that were once barely above a whisper around the table come to a complete pause when I pull out the chair. You could literally hear a pin drop if someone would. The guy whose back was originally turned to me slowly turns to see what caused the interruption. I nearly tip the chair over as I sit down. He's wearing a hunter green Henley shirt and jeans now, but it's him. *Mr. Smug Hottie.*

"Pardon me?"

Holy shit! I totally just said that last part out loud. I can feel the heat creeping up my skin, so I put my hands over my eyes and let my elbows keep me from face planting on the table.

"I can still see you, Brennan," he teases.

"What are you doing here? I thought you said you didn't work here!" I squeak. My attempt to change the course of this disaster is futile.

"Mr. Smug Hottie, huh?" My hands are still covering my eyes, but I can feel his stupid smirk. "We meet once, and you already give me a nickname. That's cute."

I wish the floor would just swallow me. Any moment now would be great. I know all eyes are really on me, so I need to shake this embarrassment off. I have to turn this around. I can't let this be how my new co-workers get introduced to me. I remove my hands and put on the best brave face I could muster.

"Well, I had changed my mind about the hottie part after you opened your smug trap, so now I just call you Mr. Smug," I huff. An audible gasp is heard through the silence.

"And here I thought we had gotten off to a good start." He tsks. "I didn't even get you caught being out there with me," he adds in a whisper. He looks around the room, and suddenly, everyone busies themselves with carrying on like before. I know they're still listening, though.

"So you never answered my question. I thought you said you didn't work here," I push, desperate to get the attention off me.

"I don't. I'm just here for the meeting."

He shrugs like it's the most logical answer ever. I was about to question him further, but I feel a tap on my shoulder. It's Tory, and she doesn't look very happy with me. *Then again, what else is new?* Her forehead has creases that threaten to crack all that foundation she's wearing. I hope she has stock in that stuff because I swear she has a department full on her face. She is about to tell me something, but then she looks over my shoulder and backs away. What the hell was that about? Why the sudden change in her pursuit to fuck with me? I was bracing myself for it. I'm not responsible for the shit that comes out of my mouth sometimes, especially when backed into a corner. I blame it on the flight or fight response. She doesn't know I've verbally sliced her tens ways from Sunday already within my internal monologue. My "IM" has saved my job many times at the Neumanns. It's my defense mechanism until you unleash my "zero fucks" mode.

I see Atticus for the first time today as he closes the conference room door and nods in this direction. Mr. Smug adjusts a black clip on his shirt that I haven't noticed until now, and an echo sounds through the room.

"Now that everyone is here, I'll get started," he announces. Get started? What the hell is he going on about?

"We have a new housekeeper here among us. I would like you all to give a warm welcome to Miss

Brennan Delavan. Brennan, can you stand please, so
those at the other end can see you?"

I swear my jaw would have hit the floor if it wasn't
attached. Of course. Why didn't I figure this out sooner? He's about twenty-five, walks around like he owns
the place, and the workers respect him because of who
he is. That's why they went back to minding their business with a single look from him. He's the owner's son!
Geesh. And I called him Mr. Smug to his face. He just
let me dig my own grave. I bet he's going to tell his father on me. It's a prime example of how my mouth gets
me into trouble.

CHAPTER 4

Silas

I WATCH AS BRENNAN MENTALLY TRIES TO PIECE together who I am. Her reluctance to stand is endearing. I had known before I suggested she do so that she didn't like to be the center of attention. I bet my other instincts about her are correct too. She got my attention this morning with those sterling gray eyes of hers that border on being completely clear. They're the most fascinating eyes I've ever seen. Then she opened that naïve mouth of hers, and I couldn't resist toying with her. The easy banter between us was a nice change of pace. I could have told her that she was poaching on my personal space—that the fourth floor of my domain stretches from midship to the forward—but I enjoyed her concern of me being caught somewhere I wasn't supposed to be a little too much. I had opened the helipad that doubles as a retractable ceiling, leading down to the third floor. I was planning to go for a swim—until she wandered out onto my deck.

"Um, hi," Brennan finally says with a timid wave after half standing. She takes her seat quicker than she stood. "So you're Mr. Lair's son?" she asks a little too loudly. Half of the room roars in hysterics while the remaining stare at her in disbelief. Surprisingly, I don't like their reaction one bit. I observe Brennan flinch, embarrassed of her assessment.

"I'm Mr. Lair, Brennan," I reply softly. She knits her fingers together, and those beautiful grays widen. She's actually quite stunning in an understated way. The baggy uniform is far from flattering, but the sweats she wore this morning gave me a glimpse at the stacked figure that is now being hidden. Her hair pulled up into that nun bun reveals her long, delicate neck and kissably soft yet pale skin. My reddened handprint would be an exquisite contrast against the paleness. Although my taste is nothing short of extravagant in many ways,

I do appreciate her simplicity. I incorporate asceticism into my life whenever I can. Flash is for the public. I have to exude wealth to ensure I attract that business. But when I'm in my domain, I like to strip myself of that persona. Yeah, I have more money than I could ever spend in my lifetime, but other than my wildly exotic taste in liquor, I strive to keep things simple. Jeans and joggers are my go-to. To hell with stuffy suits.

"As in the owner of this boat, Mr. Lair?" she confirms, bringing me back to the here and now. I nod, and her shoulders drop. She looks around the room before looking down.

"Who did you think he was?" Tory asks condescendingly from behind her. I shush her with a warning look. It doesn't help that Brennan is sitting in Tory's usual seat. Senior staff sits at this end of the table closer to me during meetings for obvious purposes. They're my leadership team. I wasn't going to let Tory make her move, though. Honestly, I don't think it's a good idea for Tory to be over her training. I can see the claws ready to come out because she feels threatened. We've fucked more than I care to admit—last night included—but I'm trying to distance myself from her now. I came to that conclusion when she kept trying to make sure it was okay she fucked my cousins. It's a troublesome indication that she thinks of us as more than what we are.

It won't be easy to wean myself from her while I'm on the cruise without alternative pussy. She knows exactly how to give me what I like. She caters to my kinkiest vices. Surprisingly, though, my attention is divided. Right now, my dick is twitching as I think of the raven-haired, naïve girl sitting next to me. I want to break her in the best way possible. I want to shatter her innocence in splintering, unrecognizable pieces.

"Sorry, sir," Brennan whispers in a voice so low, I wasn't sure if I heard her right.

"Nothing to be sorry for. Welcome to The Playboy's Lair."

I continue with the meeting, but I'm not blind. She doesn't belong here. Without someone looking out for her, she is going to get eaten alive, but I can't think about her right now. I'll talk with Atticus later. I inform the staff that we're down seven people for various reasons and that we'll need some help in the aft of the ship. I ask for volunteers. Several raise their hand, but I'm still short one person.

"We have six volunteers. We need one more person," I encourage.

"I'll do it," Brennan says timidly as she raises her hand. She stares at a spot on the table like it has the answers to world peace on it.

My rational self is screaming fuck no, but my urge to bring her over to the dark side wins out. *I can keep an eye on her better*, I reason with myself.

"Great! Way to step up, guys. I'll have just you seven stay behind, and everyone else is dismissed."

Tory lingers behind, and it doesn't go unnoticed. As the senior supervising housekeeper, she doesn't have restricted access to the aft. I don't need her to stay, though. Her stint as Brennan's trainer has been cut short.

"You can go, Tory. I only need these seven to stay," I emphasize again.

"Yes, sir," she mocks.

Yeah, it's time that she is cut off. Just because I intermittently give her some cock doesn't give her permission to be insubordinate. She'd better watch herself, or she just may find herself out on her ass. I wait until she closes the door behind her before resuming the meeting.

"How many of you have worked the aft before?" I recognize a couple of faces, but other than Brennan, I'm not sure. Four people raise their hand, so that makes the process easier. I put the two guys that I recognize in charge of getting everybody up to speed. I split them into two groups with a team leader for each. I inform them that the team with three will have another member join them later. His name is Seth, but he couldn't make it to the meeting because I currently had him covering in the kitchen.

One group will take the first floor, and one will take the second. I assign Brennan to the group responsible for the second floor since that is where I'll be.

"What will we have to do?" Brennan asks.

I see right through her nonchalant questioning. She is terrified and equal parts embarrassed by her inability to make the connection of who I was, yet she volunteered anyway. It's a true testament to her tenacity. She is an enigma I can't wait to crack. I want to know what makes her tick—where her hot spots are. *Yeah, that went south real fast.*

"The same job you would've done in the forward. Only now, you'll concentrate on the second floor. It's less work, but it's divided among a smaller team," I explain. "You will be privy to more information about what happens on that floor, so remember the NDA you signed. Your team leader will be Jacob. He will be the one to get you up to speed and train you now."

"So I ... I mean, we won't be involved in illegal sex stuff then, right?"

I swear she is too fucking cute. *Illegal sex stuff?* Why does she slide past my asshole tendencies? Anyone else would have gotten a serious ass chewing—a verbal beatdown for even asking something so stupid. The duplicity is a double-edged sword. I want to fuck and protect her at the same damn time.

"As opposed to what, the legal kind? Is that what you want? To be a participant?"

Now, I'm just fucking with her again. I can't help it. I watch as the mask of strength slips off her naked, makeup-free face. Her eyebrows nearly disappear into her hairline, and her breath hitches. My dick throbs against my jeans. I bet she is a virgin. I'd put my net worth on it. Her virginal skin beneath my hand is too much to ask of myself to resist. Goddammit to hell. She walked right into my lair of sex—a fucking virgin.

"No offense, sir, but no thank you," she squeaks out.

I don't like this version of her. The one that blends in with the other obedient workers. I like the snarky girl I met this morning who referred to me as Mr. Smug Hottie. I'm surrounded by obedience—hell, I demand it—so why do I want something different from her? Why is my little rebel such a cock tease?

"Well, in that case, Brennan, no, you don't have to be involved in any of the sex stuff," I chide. "Although, I'm really curious now as to what you think goes on back there. I don't sell sex or encourage prostitution. My operations are completely legal. I think your fantasies may be running a bit wild, miss."

She flushes crimson, and my dick jumps. My little rebel just may have a wild side. I was just kidding with the whole fantasy thing, but I may have mistakenly hit the proverbial nail on the head. If she has any untapped fantasies, I'll make it my mission to explore each one of them. Oh, this cruise just became a hell of a lot more fun.

"I don't know what to think, Mr. Lair. This all new to me. I'm up for the challenge, though."

I need to end this meeting now. If my jeans get any tighter, they will cut the circulation off to my dick. I didn't miss the hint of snark there. I want to spank her ass and then stuff that smart mouth of hers with my cock. It appears the newest member of the team is a spitfire when pushed. I'm relieved to know she is not a complete pushover because that gives me something to work with.

Yes, sir … no, sir gets old with me really quick. I need a challenge. I need a reason to make that ass glow—a reason to leave my mark in a disciplinary wake. I rarely lead one of the experiences on these cruises. We change it up every time, and my waiting list is ridiculous. I haven't taught "Intro to Erotic Spanking" since the very first cruise three years ago. Now, my restraint will be severely tested. Spanking is not just a class to me. It's an acquired taste, and it's what gets me off. Teaching techniques all day, introducing toys, and being involved in the demonstrations with the novice guests is only going to heighten my need to have my own personal playtime. Normally, I'd use Tory to satisfy that itch because she's available as my sex kitten on every cruise. Only now, I want to get acquainted with a virgin pussy and a virgin ass.

"You all are dismissed. Jacob and Henry … I need you two to take your teams to your assigned floors and get them familiarized immediately with their shift, expectations, and for the love of God, get Miss Delavan fitted for a uniform that actually fits."

I see Brennan wince at my last statement, but it's not an insult directed at her. It didn't go undetected that I'm sure Tory put Brennan in the potato sack fit. She's never had competition before. I don't bring my conquests on board with me, and I don't cross the line with my guests. I don't make it a habit to fornicate with my employees either, but Tory was on a determined mission to fuck me from the first time she stepped foot on my boat. I eventually gave in, and I'd be lying if I said she was anything less than spectacular in bed. Plus, she likes to be spanked with any and everything—both thuddy and stingy. My dick is partial to her talents and open mind. I just need to find a way to convince my brain to move on.

Everyone leaves, but as if I've conjured her up, Tory appears moments later. A distinctive click signals what she's come back for. Or did she even leave?

"What do you want, Tory?" I ask as if I don't know. "I don't appreciate your act of defiance in front of the staff."

"What defiance? What is it that I did wrong this time?" She seductively inches closer, and with each step, my resolve weakens. My dick is already hard from thoughts of Brennan and all the depraved shit that I want to do to her. At this point, I just need to bust a nut. I don't give two shits if Tory think she's winning either.

"You know what. The bitchy attitude toward the new hire ... the refusal to leave after everybody was dismissed—take your pick." With one snatch of the measly fabric that is keeping her tits from my view, the buttons go clashing against the marble. She tries to remove the shirt and jacket as one, but I still her hands.

"No need," I chastise. I turn her so that she is facing the conference table. "Assume the fucking position," I order.

I'm sure she thinks I'm in the mood to play because she's been disobedient. She puts her hands on the table in front of her and pushes her ass in my direction.

I undo her dress pants and ease them down her long sexy legs. She isn't wearing panties, as usual, and I can smell how wet she already is for me. I raise her jacket and shirt combo just enough to get a better view of her delectable tight ass.

Too bad she's not going to get the spanking I'm sure she's craving. I know her cues, and right now, she wants to feel my hand on her ass. I grab the condom from my pocket and undo my pants in a rush. This will be quick. I slide the latex down my already hard shaft and line myself up at her entrance. I waste no time slamming into her dripping wet pussy.

She backs her ass up to meet my every stroke, and I know this fuck will be even shorter than I thought. I wrap a single hand around her hair and yank as I pound into her. Her heat is so damn addicting. My balls begin to tingle, my impending orgasm so damn close. I need her to get there.

"This is your pussy, Silas," she squeals.

I can tell from the clench that she has on my cock that she is close too. I reach around her and massage her clit as I slow my strokes to the tempo that I know does it for her. I nibble on her ear, and that's all that it takes. Her fucking orgasm pulls me over—my load ripped from me like a rocket. I push her forward and piston my hips to give her every last damn drop. I let

my dick throb for a minute before I pull out and remove the condom.

"You want me to suck you clean, baby?" She knows
I hate when she tries that baby shit.

It's just a fuck. She's not mine, and I'm not her
baby. Nothing is going change that. I don't have the
time or the inclination for relationships, but if I did, it
wouldn't be her. She knows this because I was upfront
from the beginning.

"Don't!" I warn. "Let's not pretend this anything
more than a fuck—satisfying a mutual want."

I grab some Kleenex from a desk in the corner
to wrap the used condom in before shoving it in my
pocket. Yes, I'm taking it with me because I don't trust
anyone. I'm certainly not going to leave my DNA behind for someone to use to get pregnant. I definitely
wouldn't put it past Tory to try some desperate shit like
that. I wipe my dick off with the rest of the Kleenex in
my hand before tucking myself back into my jeans.

"So what now, Silas? Are you done with me? You
didn't even use your belt or your hand on me. Is it her?
Yeah, I saw the way you looked at the Mary Poppins
wannabe. Do you want to fuck her? Do you want to
replace me?" Her voice rises an octave with that last
question. She's going for the bitch act, but all I see is
desperation.

"That's enough. Don't forget your fucking place or the reason you're allowed on my yacht at all. Fucking you is just a bonus, but you're still an employee. Who I want to and who I actually fuck is of no consequence to you," I boom. I don't give two shits if I can be heard outside these walls either. "I think it's best if we bring shit back to just professional. I don't have time for anything else. This is no longer fun for me."

"Look, Silas. I'm sorry," she backpedals. "I just got jealous for a second because you were looking at her the way you used to look at me. I know that you're not mine, but I can't lose the part of you I do have."

"I don't know what part of me you think you have, but you're mistaken. You have no reason to ever be jealous. This is not anything new. We established this before I ever allowed myself to stick my dick in you."

I shake my head. I need a damn drink. This makes me think twice about getting involved with another employee. Brennan makes my dick ache, but the headache is not worth it. If Tory is this damn whipped, a virgin would probably go all stage-five clinger on my ass.

"Get your shit together," I suggest as I walk past her to unlock the door. She doesn't move from the spot that I left her. I'm not in the mood for emotional baggage. It's barely lunchtime, and I'm already heading to my room for a shot of whiskey and to wash off my dick. That Kleenex shit didn't do the job.

One shot turns into three. The sun is out now, so it's much warmer than it was this morning. I head out to the railing where Brennan stood. I chuckle to myself as I think about her persistence to get me to leave an area restricted to guests. *Fuck yeah, it's restricted to guests—employees too.* Suddenly, I want to know all about this naïve woman who has ventured into my lair. What started out as a mere favor to Thomas has piqued my interest. What is her background? How is it that a twenty-one-year-old woman has never owned a cell phone? How is she still a virgin? She is freaking gorgeous.

CHAPTER 5

Brennan

I TRY TO LISTEN ATTENTIVELY AS JACOB DISCUSSES our shifts with me and the other two co-workers, Ben and Seth. We're standing in the hallway outside some swanky club called Hedonistic Lair on the second floor. I'm the only female assigned to this floor since Regina, the only other female who volunteered, was sent to work the first floor. I manage to hear that I'll be working the evening shift—three to eleven. Can't say I'm surprised, since I have no seniority. I wish I could start early and have my evenings free.

I don't even know what the hell I was thinking when I volunteered for this gig. The aft is the very section of the boat I was trying to avoid. It's like some crazy woman possessed my body and made my hand go up. It was imperative for me to erase my first impression with Silas ... um, Mr. Lair. First, I reprimand him for being in an off-limits area to guests, and then I manage to call him smug to his face—all before mistaking him to be the son and not the actual owner of the damn boat. Raising my hand was out of some stupid, misplaced guilt, and now I can't get out of it. I'm going to have to put my big girl panties on and do whatever the hell job I foolishly volunteered for.

"Earth to the new girl back there," Jacob says, obviously annoyed that I missed something. "Can you just answer the question? We have a lot of ground to cover before tonight."

"Can you repeat the q-q-question?" I stutter, embarrassed that I was caught not paying attention.

"I asked what size you are," he repeats, letting out a flustered breath.

"Six," I answer quickly. I don't want to waste any more of our group's time. Jacob begins to scribble on his notepad.

"Scratch that. Her guesstimate is inaccurate," a

voice sounds from behind us. We all turn to see Mr. Lair walking up to us. That walk of his commands the room, and all attention is on him. Well that, and he's our boss.

"It's not a guess, sir," I reply while trying not to sound like I'm challenging him. "I really do wear a size six." *I should know.* It's my body, after all. But I don't say that last part out loud.

"Hmmm, is that so?" he asks.

His eyes are roaming my body like a gentle caress. He surprises me by grabbing a handful of my pants fabric at the hip. This makes my pants cling to my ass, revealing the hugeness of it. His knuckles graze me, and I struggle to keep my knees from buckling. I let my eyes fixate on the strong grip he has on me. The veins in the back of his hands are pronounced, and it's so damn hot. I switch the weight to my other foot to create some distance between his hand and my hip. I should be objecting to him putting hands on me, but the truth is, I wish I had more of it. I mistakenly look up and into his captivating blues. That smirk he's wearing tells me that he knows just what effect he is having on me.

"I'm a connoisseur of the female form, Miss Delavan. The ass is my specialty," he continues. "Your waist is a four, but this ass is definitely a five."

His eyes linger on my ass, and I can't help the audible gulp that escapes. My skin is on fire. The other three guys follow his gaze, and I'm appalled at my own reaction. Why am I letting this happen—letting him sexually size me up in front of everyone? Because let's face it. This conversation is so not about my clothing size. The flash of lust that I just saw is anything but professional.

"Put her in a size five, Jacob," he finishes. Just like that, he has flipped the switch back to business.

"Shall we go inside or are you all content to hold up this wall out here?" he questions, pointing at the entrance of the club.

"Sir, yes, sir," Jacob says.

The moment is gone. I don't know if I should be disgusted or flattered that he obviously likes my ass. I follow behind the group and try to keep up. I don't want to get caught not paying attention again. Mr. Lair is walking behind me, and I can't help but wonder if he's watching my ass now. I focus on the elegant décor as we pass through the foyer. More marble, but in red and gold. The space is illuminated once we pass the threshold and holy shit! What is this place? I don't realize my jaw has dropped until Seth puts a single index finger under my chin and closes it. He winks at me, but not in the "melt your panties" way that Mr. Lair does.

It was more like a mmmhmm kind of thing. My eyes don't know where to look first. Weird furniture pieces are evenly spaced around the room, and a cross looking thing is propped against the wall off to the side.

"This is where my classes occur," Mr. Lair announces, once we've all had a chance to look around the room. I'm confused even more so now.

"What do you teach in here?" I can't be the only one dumbfounded by this.

A deep belly laugh ensues. "So Jacob! I guess you haven't gotten far enough in that orientation of yours," Mr. Lair concludes.

"To be fair, sir, we all know what kind of experiences occur on this boat from the many years we've worked for you. Seth and Ben just have never worked the aft. I was waiting until we got to this area to explain what this private club is for and how to clean the equipment," he explains.

"Well, then, let me enlighten you, Miss Delavan. I offer various experiences aboard my ship for like-minded people. Each cruise usually offers only two experiences—to keep the overall setting intimate. The experiences consist of one course where invited guests learn and experiment with a new kink that is unfamiliar to them, and the other experience is for seasoned people to come together to share whatever fantasy is highlighted for that cruise. The experiences rotate every cruise, and my exclusive waiting list is only for the most elite."

I stop my jaw from dropping this time, but my nosy as shit brain won't drop it. "What two experiences are organized for this cruise?" He said he was leading the teaching one? I want to know just how kinky he is.

"Curious, are you?" He pins me with his signature stare, and everyone else disappears. I only see him. I'm seeing more of the naughty in him than I did before. The one who pins you to the spot with one glance. "Curiosity killed the cat, sweetheart." Suspiciously, I wonder which cat he is referring to?

"Um, never mind then. What do we have to clean in here?" I ask, trying to change the subject and get the attention off me.

"The course I mentor is an introduction to impact play, since I'm sure that's your real question."

Of course, he isn't going to let me get away with it. I think he likes to put me on the spot. I look away, so I'm caught off guard when he grabs my hand and pulls me toward a cabinet located in the back of the room. Our group follows. He lets go of my hand to open it, and I can't for the life of me look away.

"These are my toys, Brennan. They're all for different types of spanking."

"Damn." I hear a voice so low I'm not sure everyone heard it. It was Seth. The cabinet is filled with paddles, whips, and more shit I don't recognize hanging on hooks. He pulls out some concealed drawers and even more kinky shit come into view.

"Jacob will give you the specifics on how to sanitize everything, but more importantly, how to put things back in their rightful place. Members sign up for personal playtime with their partners in one of ten parlor areas. These rooms need to be cleaned as well. While the rooms are occupied, you will each serve as liaisons to non-aft staff to bring the guests things they've ordered such as drinks or food. You will keep track of their allotted scheduled time in order to know when to clean the private parlors. They must be cleaned between each guest's use."

Mr. Lair dismisses us after that bomb he just dropped on us. This is so out my comfort zone that I may as well not even be in a zone at all. *Holy mess.* I've managed to put myself squarely in the middle of the kinky crap I was trying avoid. I have to serve these people? During their private *play*time? We all know what that private time means. I didn't even bother asking what the other experience was. I don't even fully grasp the whole spanking concept. Who wants to be spanked on purpose? And as an adult? Rich people really are weird. I'm lucky my brain hasn't exploded yet with what he did share. *Smug bastard.* He knew exactly what I really wanted to know, and he called me on it.

"Earth to Brennan again," Jacob chastises. The boss has left the room, so he is back to his annoying self. "I said the uniforms would be delivered to your room later this afternoon. The experiences don't start until tomorrow morning. Mr. Lair likes to let everyone settle in before things kick off. That being said, we'll meet back here at six for a run-through of what to clean and with what. Seth and Brennan will take the evening shift starting tomorrow, and Ben and I will work during the day." He tells us to enjoy the rest of our afternoon.

"Well, looks like it's me and you, girlfriend," Seth says in an exaggerated fashion after the other two leave. I knew from the moment I saw him that he was gay. He's so gorgeous with defined muscles that would make any woman look twice. He's too good looking for this job—too bad he's batting for the other team. His thick eyebrows and naturally long lashes are amazing, and I don't even care about girly stuff like that. He's in his mid-twenties too, if I had to guess, which is my thing. I like to guess people's age. No reason, in partic-ular, just my quirk.

"I would rather work with you anyway, honey.

Those other two are cool but have a major stick in their asses." I laugh at his assessment because it's pretty spot-on. Yup! Seth and I will get along just fine.

"You won't get an argument from me there," I assure him. "I'd rather work with you too."

"Now for the real. Did you see how that fine ass man was looking at you the entire time? I swear my own cock jumped to attention when he grabbed your pants. I was like ... dayum! All that testosterone."

I can't help but giggle. "Shut up, Seth. He did no such thing. He was just trying to make a point. He wasn't staring at me the entire time, either. I'm like in a non-existence league when it comes to that man because I'm so far out of his, it's laughable."

"Girl, your naïvety is so damn cute, but you need to get a clue. That man sees past those baggy clothes and plain Jane look you have going on. I see it, and I'm not even into pussy. You're a rare find, baby girl, and I'd bet any kind of money that you're on his radar. Out of his league, my ass."

He rolls his eyes, and I fall to the floor in hysterics. He just stands there looking at me like I've lost my damn mind, which makes me laugh even harder. I have a mirror. I know what I look like compared to women like Bosom Barbie. He's giving me way too much credit. I guess we all need friends who boost our ego, though. He doesn't know it yet, but I'm declaring him my new best friend. I've never had one of those before.

"Get up, crazy girl. Let's go grab some food and discuss your makeover." He pulls me up, and we link arms.

"No makeover, Seth. I'm comfortable being me," I say.

"Whatever. We'll see, Miss Delavan," he mocks in his best Mr. Lair's voice. I'm laughing so hard now that tears roll down my cheeks. I haven't laughed this much in … well, ever.

This evening was great with Seth. I could feel a real friendship forming. It's easy being around him, and he makes me laugh. We swapped stories about our background, and he is even more determined to pull me out of my shell. I haven't lived at all, according to him, and he wants to put a giant size hole in my verdant bubble. I'm not that innocent … geez. He's an only child and started working with Mr. Lair two years ago. He's held several different jobs, but a friend that no longer works here got him this job. He saw it as a way to travel the world while he was still young enough to do so. He couldn't afford these trips otherwise—much like me.

He's twenty-five, just like I estimated. He gave me

the scoop on Tory and how they all think she slept her way to the top. She was the youngest before I arrived and was the one with the shortest tenure, yet she holds a leadership position. Seth has no doubts that she's jealous of me if how Mr. Lair looked at me today was any indication. Even though I do know he checked out my ass, that was just a human male response. I'm sure he's not lusting after me. Especially now that I know he's hooked up with Tory and probably still does. Who would downgrade from that? It's not that I have a low self-esteem either; I'm just realistic.

I finally make it back to my cabin after an entertaining afternoon with Seth and more training with the group. We all ate dinner in the third-floor lounge, where I recognized some of the people from today's meeting. No Tory, however. She's probably busy with Mr. Lair. I don't want to think about that, though. I just want to shower and decide what I'm going to do before my afternoon shift tomorrow besides reading the novel-sized training manual Jacob gave me tonight.

I flick the light on in my room, and my eyes roam right past the garment bag hanging from the closet. I'm guessing my new uniform has been dropped off. No, my attention is on the iPhone box sitting on my bed. Just because I've never owned a phone doesn't mean I don't know what one looks like. I rush to the bed to peel off the sticky note attached. Addressed to me, the note is from Mr. Lair.

Brennan, here is a company phone that you'll now need since you're working in the aft. I've taken the liberty of adding a few apps I think you may enjoy. FYI, I'm still baffled by how a twenty-one-year-old has never owned a phone ;) Don't worry ... there's an instruction manual. Oh, and guess what? There's a camera on the phone that doesn't even need film. It's one of those digital ones. Welcome to the 21st century ...

LOL,

Mr. Smug Hottie a.k.a. Silas

CHAPTER 6

Silas

I STAND AGAINST THE RAIL, LOOKING OUT INTO THE night as the ocean laps against the boat. I glance at my watch and wonder if Brennan has reached her room yet. A smile forms on my lips just thinking about her reaction to my gift and, more importantly, my note. Hell, I've never had this much interaction with my employees before, other than Tory. Tonight, I had Atticus issue iPhones to all of them—all so it wouldn't look preferential to give one to her. I've never given out company phones before. The unlimited Wi-Fi needed to text has always been a perk of senior leadership, but I just extended this perk to include my aft staff. Although I did insist on delivering hers myself. That earned me a curious look from my house manager.

With a glass of Macallan in one hand and my phone in the other, I take my inappropriateness a step further. *I text Brennan.*

Me: *Have you figured out how to use the phone yet? - Mr. Smug Hottie*

Several minutes pass. Just when I think that I won't get a response tonight, I see those three dots appear. She's typing. I take a few swigs of the scotch in my glass as I wait patiently.

Brennan: *You aren't going to let me live that down, are you?*

Me: *Not a chance! Where would the fun be in that?*

Brennan: *Thank you for the phone. It's nice to be a part of the 21st century (insert eye roll). The camera is really nice just like you said. I've been playing with it for the past hour, learning all the cool features. I hope that's okay. I know it's supposed to be for business. It's just so amazing—it's a computer inside the phone.*

I can't help but laugh over her obvious enthusiasm. It makes all the scheming just to get her a phone totally worth it. Her response is sweet with a hint of smartass and naïve all rolled into one.

Me: *The phone is yours to do with as you please. Have you had a chance to check out the Spotify app I added? You don't have to keep the songs. Just thought I'd add a few so you could get the hang of how to make playlists.*

Brennan: *Yes. I love the app and all three songs. I especially love the "Tonight" song by Nonso Amadi. I was listening to it on repeat before I got your message.*

That song is one of my favorites too. She has good taste. I know I'm breaching dangerous territory here, and I should leave her alone, but she is intriguing. She's an anomaly of fresh air—untainted. Is that why she appeals to me? I want to dirty her up in the best possible way—beneath me and stuffed full of my cock. My restraint is being tested, and so far, I'm failing miserably. Might as well continue down that road—at least for tonight.

Me: *I know you were checking out the indoor pool this morning. Want to join me for a midnight swim?*

I hit send before I can talk some sense into myself. I'm crossing so many lines, and I can't say that I give a shit. I make the rules. Several minutes pass with no answer, and I must say I'm not used to being on this side of the fence. Can't say that I like it, either. She has me anxious like a nervous schoolgirl until finally, I see those long-awaited three dots again. *Thank fuck.*

Brennan: *To be honest, swimming is kind of my thing. It's a long story, but I try to do it daily. That's why I was checking it out this morning. If you promise that it's just swimming, then I would love to join you. I don't work tomorrow until the afternoon shift.*

So she wants to lay down the rules, huh? *If I promise it's just swimming?* How cute—charming even. I'll play along for a bit, but she has no idea she just awakened my competitive nature with that little ultimatum. I make the rules, and I always get what I want. Let's see how she responds once the kid gloves are off.

Me: *Of course, it's just swimming! What did you think swimming was code for? I usually swim daily too ... before sunrise. I missed today, so I thought I'd get some laps in before bed. I'll meet you at the pool in twenty minutes.*

Brennan: *Okay. See you there.*

I finish the remainder of my scotch and head to put on a pair of swim trunks. This should be fun. I'd be lying if I said I wasn't just a tad excited to see the flesh that she keeps hidden under those baggy clothes.

I arrive at the indoor pool first, so I use this time to start laying my seductive foundation. Nothing is ever as it seems. I will let her think she is setting the pace for our interactions when, in reality, I'm the mastermind pulling the strings behind the scenes. I quickly create a unique playlist and input it into the elaborate sound system built into the wall. This private feature must be accessed through a hidden control panel via the keypad. Usually, I use the music to fuel my workout when I'm doing laps in the pool. But tonight, it'll serve a different purpose.

"You know I got a special spot to help you remember me" sounds from the speaker just as Brennan enters. Her face lights up with the most earth-shattering smile as she recognizes the "Tonight" song by Nonso Amadi we were just talking about.

She's wearing an enormous white t-shirt with cartoon characters on it. It's the most adorable thing I've seen in a long time. Most women—hell, scratch that ... any other woman would have worn the smallest bikini they could find to get my attention. Her shirt comes down to her knees. I walk over to her like her attire isn't out of the norm.

"Like the music choice?" I ask, already knowing the answer.

"I do," she beams. "Where is the music coming from?"

I point at the area next to the stairs that leads to

the next level. I have the panel flipped open so she could see. "It's one of my secret gizmos," I reply.

"I have to say this boat is filled with surprises," she says more to herself.

"Come on! Let's go swim," I suggest.

Her freakish gray eyes widen as I pull my shirt over my head. Her fingers lock together as I make a show of sliding my joggers down my legs to reveal my swim trunks. She lets her eyes travel south for the briefest of seconds before turning away from me. *Too late, sweetheart.* That lovely shade of red your skin is now wearing tells me all I need to know. She is definitely a virgin. I run and jump into the cool water to combat my growing erection. I freestyle for a few strokes before I re-emerge.

"Come on in. The water feels great," I encourage.

She walks to edge and dips her toe in before jumping in feet first. She swims until she meets me in the center of the pool. She shakes the water from her face as she treads the eight feet. Her bun tumbles loose, and it's my turn to stare. Her raven locks are still constrained by the elastic holding it together, but the length flows away from her as her shirt floats up to her chest. I peruse her from head to toe. I see why she's wearing that shirt. Her one piece is a couple of sizes too small. Her ass is so damn nice. Even through the water, I can see its heart-shaped perfection. My palm itches to reach out and grab it, and I can feel my dick trying to harden again.

"Want to race?" she asks, interrupting my lustful pondering. *Yeah, sure, that's what I want to do.*

"Go!" I shout as I get a head start toward the end of the pool. With every stroke, I can hear her slicing through the water behind me, trying desperately to catch up. I touch the wall first and wait for her. My little stunt did very little to work my erection down.

"You cheated!" she accuses when she reaches me. She attempts to grab the wall behind me, but her reach falls short. Her hand grips my shoulder instead, and I pull her close merely to keep her upright since we're both standing in the shallow end now. The trouble is, I pull her right into my hardness. A moan slips past those innocent lips of hers, and the last of my restraint shatters like glass. I capture her lips and work the seam until she opens them for me. My tongue savors hers with a fervor that surprises her. I feel a slight hesitation in her body, but it doesn't last long. She claws at me, trying to deepen the kiss and, oh, do I oblige.

"Shit," I growl as I lift her legs around my waist. My hands slide down her bare ass not covered by her one piece, and I waste no time pushing her further against my cock. My fingers are so close to her pussy. I just want a taste. My dick pushes against the thin fabric keeping her pussy from me. I rub her against it, desperate for the friction to stave off some of the ache. She whimpers, and all thoughts of taking her slowly are getting foggy.

"Fuck," I curse again to myself. Brennan breaks our kiss and slides down my body, jilted.

"I'm sorry. I don't know what came over me," she apologizes. Is she fucking for real? She didn't do anything wrong. "I need to go," she adds.

I know that if she leaves now, things will be awkward between us from here on out. I grab her hand to keep her from leaving. "You have nothing to apologize for Brennan," I assure her.

"But you're my boss, and I just kissed you," she insists, embarrassed.

"Wrong! I kissed you, and I'd do it again. We're both adults." Besides that, she's omitting the fact that we took things past first base. "Come on. Let's go up a level and look out at the ocean. If you liked the view this morning, you'll love the view at night. It's my favorite."

"I really should get going," she says. She pulls her hand out of mine, knotting her fingers together, and I know she is questioning what she should do. I've come to correlate the knotting of her fingers together as something she does when she's nervous.

"Just one drink. I don't want things to end weird, okay? We'll just talk. That's it."

"Just talk?" she questions, unsure. There she goes again with the establishing rules thing. I'll allow it for now.

"Pinky swear," I promise as I untangle her fingers and hook my pinky with hers. That earns me a half smile. *That's better.*

"Okay," she finally agrees. I jump out of the pool first like a giddy schoolboy and then turn to help her out, but she has already headed for the end of the pool near the stairs that leads up to my level.

She pulls the t-shirt that now clings to her body over her head and lays it over the railing. I know I'm in trouble when I get my first true glimpse of her body. It is nothing short of every man's fucking fantasy. D cup breast, a narrow waist that leads to a heart-shaped ass, and virgin pussy. I want to claim every inch of her, explore every curve. She follows up with pulling the elastic from her hair and lets it fall to her waist. All I want to do is wrap my fist around it and claim her virtue. This image of her will be ingrained into my brain for sure. I grab a couple of towels and wrap the first one around my waist to hide my semi-erect cock before I walk over to meet her at the steps.

"Thank you," she says as she unsuccessfully tries to adjust her swimsuit to cover more of her shapely ass. I want to comment so badly about how small her fucking swimsuit is, but I refrain. I won't risk her changing her mind about having that drink with me. I envy her towel as I watch like a creeper while she quickly dries herself before wrapping it around herself.

"I'll just leave my shirt here on the rail of the stairs to dry until I come back down," she tells me. I just nod and gesture for her to lead the way. I'm absolutely watching the sway of her ass in that towel as she turns to do just that.

The night air is a little chilly for January, so I have her follow me to the fire pit located closer to the doors of my suite. Can't wait for the warmer temps as we get further out into the Caribbean Sea.

"I didn't see this here earlier," she says puzzled.

"Um, because you were too busy laying down the law." I chuckle. She does have a sort of bossy side to her, come to think of it. "That is my room, Brennan," I inform, pointing past the fire pit. "This whole fourth level, forward to midship, is my personal space."

I watch with amusement as realization dawns on her.

"Wait. So I was trespassing on your deck ... I was the one somewhere I wasn't supposed to be this morning? Why didn't you tell me?"

"Well, then, I would have had to tell you who I was." I shrug playfully.

"Yeah, about that. You let me make a total fool out of myself. I'm sure your other employees think I'm a complete whack job!" She folds her arms and huffs.

"Don't get yourself worked up. It was cute. It was way more fun to be Mr. Smug Hottie anyway."

She flushes crimson for the millionth time, and I'm beginning to like the color on her. "I'm going to grab us a couple of warm throw blankets and make us a drink."

I gesture for her to have a seat then light the fire pit before leaving. I bring back two glasses of some of my finest scotch—the Macallan 64 that I was drinking earlier when I started texting her.

"How did you know what I'd like to drink?" she asks teasingly. "You didn't even ask."

"Hmmm, aside from soda, I don't have any of that froufrou girly drink crap." I wink. "Of course, if you don't think you can't handle the manly stuff, I can order you something. What do you drink?"

"I don't drink, so I wouldn't know where to begin. Sure, I've tasted alcohol at one of the Neumann's ritzy parties, but don't ask me what it was," she snorts. She quickly covers her face, but I remove her hands and place the scotch in one hand. I take a seat across from her so that I can admire her beauty highlighted by the flames.

She gulps her first sip and wrinkles her nose in disgust. "That burns going down," she notes.

"Try sipping it, sweetheart, not deep throating it." Her eyebrows rise, and I mentally pat myself on the back—points for shock value. "It's fine liquor. It's not a shot. You're supposed to sip it."

I keep talking in hopes she'll forget about the deep throat thing. I'm supposed to be taking her slow. That comment wasn't very professional, but neither was my tongue down her throat or grinding her virginal pussy against my cock.

"What is this?" she asks while taking a careful sip this time. "It's actually okay once you get past the burn."

"Just okay? You have thousands of dollars' worth of liquor in your mouth right now. Many would kill for that sip." I love fucking with her. I would rather be *fucking* her or have her mouth full of my cum, but I will get my chance.

"Thousands? What do mean? How much is that bottle?" She picks up the bottle to inspect it. Like there would be an actual price tag on it. I can barely contain my laughter. She is just too damn adorable for words.

"Well, that bottle in your hands cost me almost a half a million," I answer truthfully. She sets the bottle back down on the table like she is afraid she may break it.

"You're lying," she accuses.

"Afraid not. What can I say? I enjoy fine scotch."

"And you're just drinking it like it's nothing. It's not even a special occasion. That's pretty pretentious, Mr. Lair."

The way she addresses me has a different tone. Not the "your my boss, Mr. Lair" tone either. Whatever it is, I like it. She leans back in the lounge chair and takes slow sips from her glass.

"So you wanted to talk. Tell me about you. How did you end up with more money than you know what to do with?" The alcohol is definitely getting to her. That was a bold question coming from her.

"Well, the short version is my paternal side has always had money dating back from their oil business. My father used his inheritance to start a few hotel chains. I inherited my share of the money when I turned twenty-one, and then what he left me when I died a few years later. My mom died when I was six. My father remarried when I graduated high school, but his iron-clad prenup ensured that she left with what she came with—nothing—so it all went to me.

Sex sells, and I'm good at it, so I decided to use it to make a profit. I'm in the sexually oriented business of bringing like-minded people together to enjoy their kink. The end." I grin.

I gave her the CliffsNotes version. She doesn't need to know the sordid details—or about Jasper. She empties her glass, so I refill it. She doesn't push for more, but I can see the unanswered questions swirling through that cute head of hers. Her inquisitive facial expressions give away her thoughts. Her wrinkled forehead and that bow above her lip show me that she is pondering something.

"What about you?" I ask.

"What about me? I don't have any money."

"Tell me about you. How is it that a twenty-one-year-old woman has never owned a phone? Tell me about your life growing up."

"My story is not as glamorous as yours, but I'll bore you with it anyway," she jokes.

She tells me that she never had a chance to meet her father. That he died before she was born. She talks about her mom and how swimming was their nightly thing before she took her own life. Her eyes sadden as she recalls that day and again when she tells me how mean the kids were when she tried to attend one of those "fancy private schools." The staff at the

Neumanns were her family as well as her friends. She didn't need frivolous things such as a phone when she didn't have anyone to call outside that house. She was homeschooled, so as she grew up, she missed out on virtually every aspect of socialization.

CHAPTER 7

Brennan

I LEAN BACK FURTHER AGAINST THE CHAIR AND LET my body relax into the cushions as the sudden euphoric feeling consumes me. The scotch has creeped up on me. One minute, I was fine, and now, my body feels light as though I'm floating. That and I can't erase this goofy smile off my face. Naughty thoughts of sitting on Silas's lap and feeling his hardness again are competing with any logic I may have about calling it a night.

"A penny for your thoughts, Miss Delavan?" Silas smirks at me knowingly.

This whole night has been one bad decision after another from the moment I got the phone he gifted me—from the moment I responded to his text. The truth is, I've never felt more alive. I've always been a rule follower, and I've certainly never been tempted to just let go of my own established rules. My rules protect me from men like him—rich, gorgeous, and powerful. I'm smart enough to know that allowing myself to get mixed up with him will not end well for me.

"Only a penny, Mr. Lair? Surely, you could do better than that," I mock. I don't know what the hell I'm doing, but I like it. I'll worry about the consequences tomorrow.

Silas stands and lets the towel he has wrapped around his waist fall effortlessly to the ground. My eyes immediately narrow in on the thick package gorging from his trunks that he makes no effort to hide.

"Tsk-tsk, sweetheart. Be careful of the game you start. Don't throw out innuendos that you don't want me to take literally. If you want that pussy of yours to remain virginal, I advise you to stand down." He winks.

Holy fuck on a stick. I wasn't expecting his direct threat. My pussy clenches, and it surprises me just how turned on I am right now. How does he know that I'm a virgin? Does he know how badly I want him to rectify that? Geez, what am I even saying? My brain has aborted all rationalization.

"Umm ... uh ... who says that I'm a virgin?" I finally get out. "You can't just assume stuff like that."

Gah, this is definitely a face palm moment. That's my snappy comeback? *How lame.* I grip my empty glass tighter, hoping to give nothing away. He doesn't answer right away. Instead, he joins me on the loveseat, pouring me a third glass of the liquid courage. The flames from the fire pit illuminate the lust in his hooded eyes. He grabs my knee, and I force myself to remain unaffected. He slides that same hand slowly upward, and my knees lock. Only now I've trapped his hand inside my thighs, mere inches from my pussy.

"Tell me, Brennan," he whispers next to me. "Have you ever been touched like this? Is your pussy craving for my fingers to come closer? Do you want them to get lost in that sweet wetness that I smell?"

I want to be appalled ... I really do. He's my boss, for God's sake. But he's right. My panties are soaked. His filthy forward talk has me wanting things I shouldn't. Things I can't admit to out loud. I grab his wrist with trembling fingers because I'm scared he may continue his travels north.

"I don't want anything," I lie. "And I don't have to

answer that question. You're my boss." My indecisiveness is giving me whiplash. I'm leading him on, yet I can't help it.

"Mere words. Don't ever lie to me. That question was rhetorical. I know exactly what that tight little cunt wants. I'm the master of these types of games, love. You want me to chase ... to beg ... to be the pursuer? I won't. I only fuck what's offered freely; if I choose to accept. So go ahead. Deny what you're feeling right now. Hide behind the 'I'm your boss' cloak. Just know you're the only one who believes that."

He removes his hand from between my legs and pours himself another glass of scotch like he just didn't issue that verbal slap. I didn't ask him to pursue me or any of the other crap he just said. I feel like I've been doused with a bucket of ice water. How dare I step out my league? I should have never agreed to come up for a swim and definitely not joined him for a drink in to his personal space. So much for not leaving things on an awkward note.

"And with that, it really is time for me to go," I say as I stand. I sway and have to grab the back of the loveseat to remain upright. I may be a little more than just buzzed. Silas quickly stands too, ready to offer me his hand. "I got it." I refuse to let him help me after he basically told me I wasn't worth chasing.

I stumble past him and head to my room. Silas follows closely behind me until I make it safely down the stairs. Neither of us says anything more, and I'm kind of disappointed he is letting our night end this way. Oh well, back to reality.

The alarm on my phone goes off next to my head, and I groan. I can't believe it's eight a.m. already. I was out until one with Silas, but sleeping in didn't help. My head feels like elves are tap dancing on my forehead, my mouth is dry, and my stomach is roiling every time I move. At least the phone alarm is less offensive than the one from yesterday.

I slowly reach for the button located above the nightstand and press it to electronically open the curtains. The room floods with instant light, and I have to blink a few times before my eyes accommodate to the intrusion. It is then that I see orange juice next to my bed and two aspirins. There is a note, but it simply says, "Take me," with no signature. It must be Silas. Only he would know the hell I'm in at this moment, but how did he get in here? And without me knowing? I take the pills and drink just enough juice swallow them. I spot the bottle of water next to where the juice was sitting, but my stomach is protesting the thought of any of it.

Within ten minutes, I'm hovering over the toilet and dry heaving. I've already thrown up the little that was in my stomach. I hear a knock on my door, but I can't lift my head from the porcelain to care. I'm not scheduled to work for another seven hours, so I'm not obligated to be bothered with anything work related. I'm content to ignore whoever it is until I hear the distinctive beep of a key card being inserted and then my door opening.

"Brennan?" Silas calls. *Ugh.* This day just went from bad to worse. Maybe if I don't answer, he'll go away. How dare he let himself into my room? *Again.* I dry heave once more just as he opens the door to find me kneeling on the floor. "Shit, Brennan." He curses.

"Go away," I manage to say between hurls. I know I look completely disgusting, and he's witnessing me at my worst.

"Cut the tough shit because I'm not going anywhere. I should have never let you drink that much. If I had to guess, I'd say you've never been drunk before either." I turn slightly to see him shaking his head. Well, fuck him.

"What happened to not chasing or pursuing me? Why are you here? I can take care of myself."

"I'm not doing either. You're doing a fine job, by

the way, of the taking care of yourself bit," he rebuts just as snarky.

"Fuck you, y-y-you jerk!" I snap. Yup, I just cursed out my boss. There goes my job. I regret the words as soon as they're out. I'm usually better at holding my tongue. I had years of practice at the Neumann's ... well, mostly with Mrs. Neumann. Silas surprises me, though, with a hearty laugh that fills the small confines of my bathroom.

"In time, sweets. Today is not that day. Let's concentrate on one thing at a time," he quips.

"You're impossible." I don't elaborate because I can't win with him. His whiplash tendencies are just as bad as mine are. He is so mercurial.

"Impossible to resist. Yes, I know. I hear that all the time." He chuckles while I huff in frustration. He walks over to my shower and turns the water on.

"What are you doing?" I panic.

"Well, I figured you might want to wash away that puke you're wearing."

I look down, and sure enough, I have a few chunks on my leg that missed the toilet. "Ugh," I groan. "Just shoot me now." And if that wasn't enough, I just realized I'm on the floor in just a t-shirt and panties. I really am a mess right now. All my dignity just went poof in a puff of smoke.

"Don't be embarrassed. We've all been there at one point in our lives. Just admit that this is a first for you."

"Fine. I've never gotten that buzzed before, and now I'm paying for it. Happy now?"

"Oh, sweetheart, you were wayyyyyy past buzzed. You drove straight past buzz fest and into drunkville. What you're experiencing now is called a hangover," he informs me. "I have no reason to be happy about this. I can think of quite a few other firsts of yours that I will enjoy, but this isn't one of them."

I know one of the "firsts" he's hinting at, but he just said quite a few. What other firsts is he talking about?

"You're pretty sure of yourself for a guy who swore he wouldn't pursue me. I remember that, so I guess I wasn't too drunk."

"So you're admitting that you're a virgin?"

"Whatever. It's not like it's a big deal. Yes, I'm a virgin. There, I've said it even though it's none your business. My sex life, or lack thereof, has nothing to do with this job." I push myself up off the toilet. I couldn't be even more ashamed if I tried so no use in just sitting on the floor.

"I'm going to enjoy filling that smart mouth of yours with my cock just as much as I will enjoy making your ass red." That sexy smirk of his is back, and I have no doubt he means every word. I have to look away.

My stupid body is reacting to him even with being sick.

"Are you crazy or something because I can't keep up?" I take it back. His whiplash rivals mine. He's cuckoo for Cocoa Puffs cray. He is all over the place. One minute, he swears he's not going to chase me, and the next minute, he's in my room telling me what he's going to enjoy doing to me. I just have to resist being pulled under his spell again.

"Take your shower, Brennan," he instructs. The change in his tone throws me off as a sharpness lingers in the air as a finality. He leaves me standing there and closes the door behind him. I get into the shower, dumbfounded on what just happened.

I spend at least a half an hour in the shower trying to make myself feel human again. After washing my hair, I'm exhausted. My headache is finally dissipating, but I'm weak, and my stomach still feels sick. I have no idea if Silas is still here, but dammit, my clothes are out there. I step out of the shower and wrap one of the bath towels around me. I peek my head out of the bathroom, and there he is—sitting on the empty bed, opposite of mine. He points at the t-shirt and joggers he's laid out on my bed. I was wrong. It is possible to be even more embarrassed. If he's set clothes out for me, that means he went through my things—my ratty, secondhand things.

"What are you still doing here?" I ask in an attempt to appear unfazed.

"Brennan, where are the rest of your clothes?" And there it is. The ultimate gut punch. It's not the first nor will it be the last time that someone looks down their snobby nose at my clothes. I'm not quite reading that vibe from him, but the judgment is there all the same.

"Why do you always answer a question with a question, *Silas*?"

Trying to change the subject is futile. His stupid handsome face frowns. I try to walk over and snatch the clothes off the bed, but he beats me to it. He grabs me by the wrist and swings me around to face him. I hold on to the towel with my other hand to keep it from falling.

"Answer me. Why don't you have clothes? Why is everything in your suitcase at least two to three sizes too big? Didn't that last job pay you?"

"Which question do you want me to answer first, *boss*?" I smart off. I can feel the tears threatening to fall, and my throat gets tight.

"Don't deflect. I'm just concerned. I need to know that they paid you fairly," he growls.

"They paid me, Silas. Just leave it, please. I've put my money into savings. The things you took it upon yourself to rummage through belonged to my mother.

I don't need more than that. I don't live beyond my means."

He drops my wrist and doesn't push the issue further. "Get dressed. I'm going to order food."

I grab the clothes he set out for me and take them back to the bathroom. I notice a little late that he didn't include a bra or panties. I wasn't wearing a bra to begin with, and I'm not putting the same panties back on, so the way I see it, I have two options. I can either just put these clothes on and forego the undergarments, or I can go back out there and dig through my suitcase and face even more embarrassment. The decision is a no-brainer. I throw on the clothes and walk out just as he is ending the call with room service.

"Thank you for checking on me, Mr. Lair. I do appreciate it."

"Nice try, sweetheart. I see we're back to the Mr. Lair bit, but I'm not going anywhere. You didn't even drink the water I left for you to rehydrate. I got you drunk, and now, I'm going to take care of you. I've ordered you a light breakfast of eggs, coffee, and toast. I'm here to make sure you eat."

"I don't need a babysitter," I smart off, inserting an eye roll to give my sarcasm weight.

"Good because I'm not in the business of babysitting," he says, handing me the bottle of water. He waits until I take the bottle from him before he smacks my ass—hard. I'm caught so off guard I don't know how to react. The sting lingers, but something unexpected happens. My pussy throbs ... like really throbs. It's like the vibrations traversed to my vagina. *What the hell?*

"Hmmm. Interesting," Silas mumbles to himself.

"I'm not into that spanking kinky stuff you're into," I warn. *Or am I?*

"Mmmhmm. Drink the water, sweetheart," he says, unconvinced. "I'm going to take a quick shower. Listen for the food to arrive. I ordered for me too."

I assume he's going back to his room until he goes into my bathroom and shuts the door. I hear the shower turn on, and once again, I'm dumbfounded. I'm still standing in the center of the room speechless with the damn water bottle in my hand when he reopens the door enough to peek around it.

"Listen for Atticus too. He's bringing me clothes to change into." With that bomb, he disappears back into the bathroom. He loves dropping these little "what the fuck" bombs that render you stupefied and wondering what the hell just happened.

This is truly a *"what the fuck"* moment. Atticus is going to think I'm already fucking the boss and all by the third day. This man is going to drive me insane and leave my reputation in the toilet.

CHAPTER 8

Brennan

A FEW TAPS ON MY DOOR AND I'M HOPING IT'S the food. I begrudgingly get up to open it, and just my luck, it's Atticus.

"Morning, Miss Delavan," he greets me as if delivering clothes to his boss in one of the housekeeper's rooms is the most normal thing in the world.

"Morning," I bid him in return. I can pretend too.

"Are you getting acclimated okay?" His eyes wander around the room to gather evidence that Silas and

I just finished a romp session, I'm sure. The shower stops, and his eyes return to mine. Awkwardness permeates the air.

"So far everything has been going smoothly," I say in a rush. I don't even know why I'm so nervous. It's not even how it looks.

"Well, let me know if you need anything. See that Mr. Lair gets this." He smiles as he passes me a Gucci shopping bag.

"Will do," I assure. He nods and backs out of the door. I walk over and set the fancy gold foiled, brown bag down on the empty bed Silas occupied earlier. I'm tempted to look at what's all inside when he emerges from that bathroom wearing only a bath towel.

Fucking hell, sweet baby Jesus. Rivulets of water trail down his naked torso and disappear into his towel. I visually count each etch of his six pack. His towel hangs unnecessarily low, exposing the veins that lead to his thickness bulging from the plush white fabric. The sun shining through the curtains gives me my first real look at the sleeve on his right arm. I thought it was badass at the pool last night—added to his sex appeal—but now I can see all the detail. I wonder about the meaning of it. It definitely ups his hotness factor, if that's even possible.

"Can you speed up eye fucking me so that you can

pass me the bag?" He smirks. *Busted.*

"I'm not," I lie. I so am.

I grab the bag from the bed and walk it over to him except I can't look him in the eyes. I focus on his outstretched arm with the sleeve, and that proves to be yet another mistake. More veins. His arms and chest are simply swoonworthy, but the vascularity of his veins within his V adds to his virility. It makes me want to lick the path to where they lead.

"I hate to break it to you, but you're not very subtle. Quite the opposite, in fact."

He takes the bag from me since I fail to actually hand it to him. Gah, you'd swear I've never seen a man before. I have. Just nothing that even remotely compares to this man. He turns away from me and lets his towel drop as he heads back into the bathroom. I don't even pretend not to watch. He has a really nice ass. The knock on the door jolts me from my lustful stupor. This time, I'm sure it's the food. I open the door, and I couldn't have been more surprised if I tried. A lump forms in my throat in absolute fear. It's Tory, and she is pushing the cart with our food.

"Morning, Brennan," she half-ass greets. She pushes past me with the cart without being invited in.

"I didn't know that you delivered food to the rooms," I say snottily. I couldn't resist the taunt. She has been a bitch to me since we've met. Also, I want her gone before Silas comes out. Maybe my rudeness will make her leave.

"Oh, cute. I don't usually deliver food. I was coming by to see how you were handling things with your new assignment and met up with Dominic outside. I saw the food was for your room, so I told him that I would bring it in." She flips her hair in her telltale "I'm better than you" fashion.

"You think you've ordered enough stuff? All that is going to go straight to your ass," she warns as she looks horrified at the silver domes of covered food. I'm seconds away from telling her to get the fuck out of my room when Silas chooses this moment to come out of the bathroom—only half dressed. If my reputation wasn't doomed before, it sure as hell is now. Tory's jaw drops as she looks back and forth between us with obvious disdain.

Silas strides over to my mirror and runs his hands through his still wet, tousled hair. His low hanging jeans are every bit as enticing as that damn towel. And why couldn't he put on a shirt?

"What can we do for you, Tory?" he asks without turning around. "Oh good, the food is here," he says as an afterthought.

"Really, Silas? This is what you're into now? A cross

between a hobo and—" She doesn't get to finish that sentence because Silas is in her face within seconds.

"You may not want to finish that sentence, doll." I wince at hearing him call her doll. Then I get pissed for caring. A shitstorm is brewing before me, and all I can focus on is that he called her doll?

"Or what? You'll fire me? I'm the only one on this goddamn boat who knows exactly what gets you off without being coached or taught," she screams while making air quotes.

"That's enough," he booms.

Holy shit. This is a different Silas, and I want to be as far from him as possible. I make my way over to my bed after grabbing my food off the cart. I hate that I'm the cause of the fallout between him and his … what? Fuck buddy? Girlfriend? Then I think about the fooling around we did last night, and I'm annoyed. Surely, whatever they had is over if he was with me, right?

"You're right. I'm done here." One lone tear falls before she turns on her designer stilettos and heads out the way she came. I feel bad for her. I'm not exactly a cold-hearted bitch. I recognize broken even if she is a conniving twat waffle.

I take small nibbles of my food, praying that I can keep it down. My stomach feels like a roller coaster, but eating gives me something to do besides feel awkward.

Silas grabs his omelet off the cart and comes to sit next to me on *my* bed. Suddenly, this room feels too small. We both eat in silence for several minutes until the guilt is too much.

"Sorry," I whisper.

"For what?" A single eyebrow arches in confusion. His intense stare pins me to the spot, yet he continues to eat his food.

"For, umm, messing things, umm ... up with you and Tory."

He pauses midbite. "That's nothing for you to concern yourself with. And you did nothing wrong. She came to your room and was obnoxiously rude. I will handle things with her, but you don't need to give her little performance a second thought." The finality in his voice clues me in to just let the conversation go. He doesn't want to discuss her.

"I like your key," I compliment to change the subject. I've seen this key around his neck before now, but I didn't want to pry about its significance. Too late to pull my foot out of my mouth now, though. "What does it say?"

He flips the key around, and I see the word "love" etched into the gold. He seems more like a 'love 'em and leave 'em' kind of guy rather than a 'give someone his heart' kind of guy.

"I see the wheels turning in that head of yours. I don't discuss my key," he says with a soft warning.

Now, I'm even more curious about it. His love key is a contrast to every vibe he gives off. Not to mention its simplicity. It's a gold key on a silver chain. He has millions, yet this piece of jewelry can't hold that much monetary value.

"That's fine. It's none of my business," I respond in disappointment. "I managed to eat most of the stuff you ordered, so I think I'll lie down for a bit before my shift," I hint.

This is his cue to leave. He doesn't need to feel obligated to continue caring for me because he got me drunk. I'm sure I'll be branded as the cruise slut by the time I go to work. Hell, who am I kidding? I'm positive the rumors are already spreading. Silas pulls back the covers for me, so I don't make a fuss about it. I just pass him my plate and get underneath. Why I am still surprised by anything he does baffles me. He gets under the covers with me and uses his weight to push me over.

"What the heck are you doing?" I protest.

"Shhh. I'm not going to fuck you while you're hungover, so you're safe. Let's just sleep." *What the actual fuck?* After his debacle with Tory in my room, why would he think I'd let him get his tool anywhere near me?

He slides in closer behind me and wraps an arm around my waist. I can smell my cheap Dial soap on him, and that surprisingly makes me smile. The heat of his body radiates as I allow myself to snuggle into his warmth. *Yup. This is why.* All objections cease the moment I felt him. I'm treading in deep waters here, but I don't know how much I really want the life preserver that takes me away from him.

I'm cleaning one of the private parlor rooms wearing the earbuds that came with my phone. Back at the Neumann's, I used to carry around a small radio to each room while I worked. I don't know how I've ever lived without this little piece of technology. Granted, I would have purchased a phone before now had I considered all the other attributes besides calling people. Rhianna's "Work" has me dancing while I vacuum the food crumbs from the carpet. I'm feeling way better than I did this morning.

My cuddle session with Silas may have a little do with that even though he was gone when I woke up. Thoughts of Tory and her involvement with him threaten to tarnish the memory, but I'm still flying high. I don't know why. Something about that man just makes me feel alive. So cliché, but when I'm around him, I'm more than just the help. He sees me. He challenges me with his undeniable sex appeal and filthy words.

The disappearing hum of the vacuum cleaner has me stopping in my tracks to investigate the interruption. Tory stands, leaning against the wall with the end of the plug still dangling from her talon-like manicured nails. Her resting bitch face cues me in that she's come with an agenda, and I'm pretty sure I know why. It's like my thoughts have conjured her up.

"Well, aren't we chipper this evening?" she remarks. "Silas have anything to do with that?"

"I'm just listening to music to make the work go by faster." I don't know why I'm entertaining her cattiness. While it's true I've always listened to music while I clean, it's not the sole reason for my being "chipper," as she calls it.

"Cut the shit, Brennan! Was that your plan all along—the reason for your whole 'Look at me, I'm innocent' act?"

"What the hell are you talking about?" If she's come for a fight, that's exactly what she's going to get.

"I've had my eye on you since you've arrived. Playing little miss innocent while trying to get cozy with the boss. First, you sit your ass in my assigned seat at the meeting yesterday, and now you're already trying to screw him—well, if you haven't already."

Now the pieces fit. Why the table went quiet when I sat down and what she was about to say before Silas undoubtedly gave her the look. As if there weren't enough reasons for her to hate me.

"I didn't sleep with him, Tory. He only came to check on me because I was sick. He stayed to make sure I was following his directions to feel better." I leave out the cuddling part or why I got sick in the first place. I'm choosing the high road rather than to break her spirits even if she is being a major bitch.

"Whatever. I only came here to tell you not to get your hopes up. You're the shiny new toy, so expectedly, he would take notice. We have history, and I won't let anyone or anything fuck with that." She glares at me while continuing to hole the vacuum cord between her fingers. "You and I will not have any problems," she says as a statement of fact.

She finally drops the cord, not bothering to plug it back in, before she makes her dramatic exit.

She flips her blond hair, which could easily be interpreted as a fuck-off. I just stand there stunned at the whole ordeal until Seth comes in and closes the door.

"What was that all about?" he asks. I could hear that Satan in heels, bitching about something from the parlor next door.

"Oh, yeah. Bosom Barbie came to warn me to stay away from the boss."

"You call her Bosom Barbie?" He doubles over in laughter. "That's fucking hilarious. And here, I thought I could come up with some crazy names for people."

"Kind of fitting, isn't it?" I join him in laughter, but then he stops and gets serious.

"Wait! Why did she feel the need to come all the way here to warn you away from Mr. Lair? This can't be because you took her seat next to him at that meeting."

"Ugh," I groan. "So you knew that was her seat too, huh? I've only just found out because she brought it up, but that wasn't the sole reason for her visit."

After swearing him to secrecy, I tell him about receiving the phone and how things escalated from there. I include how I got drunk and how he ended up in my shower and then my bed. Maybe I should have left out some of those details, but Seth is the closest thing I've ever had to a girlfriend, and I need advice. Should I let things play out and see where they lead, or should I heed Tory's warning to keep the peace for my job's sake?

"First of all, holy shit!" he exclaims. "Okay, now that I've gotten that out. Fuck that bitch. Don't let her dictate things between you and *Mr. Smug Hottie.*"

I'm never going to live that one down. I can't believe I called him that in front of everyone. "I don't know, Seth. What if things aren't over between them? I don't want to be part of some weird triangle crap. Hell, I don't even know if I want to be anything."

"You are only delaying the inevitable, girl. Your whole face lit up just now while talking about him. All I'm saying is don't let her get in the way of whatever is happening between you two. He obviously likes you. We all see it. He's never been this involved or even been seen this much. Hell, we've never gotten phones until you showed up. My guess is that he issued them to have a way to contact you."

My mind is blown right now. What if Seth is right? Was the phone for my benefit? It's just too much of a coincidence to think otherwise. If so, that was a little sneaky but sweet. Score one for Silas.

"Don't let him double dip, but if he's willing to let go of Satan, my vote is to give him a shot. Let yourself have some fun." He comes over and gives me a hug before imparting his wisdom. "I have to get back to work and so do you. Just remember what I said. Don't let jealousy dull your sparkle, sunshine."

And with that nugget of wisdom, he plugs my vacuum cleaner back in, and then he's gone. There was so much truth in what he said. I can't be concerned about their history together. All that matters now is what they have now, and whether I'm willing to get involved with my boss. I'm torn. I know that professionalism should be at the forefront, but look where it's gotten me so far. Sometimes I don't even feel like I'm living—I feel that I'm simply existing. Silas makes me feel alive and free. Maybe taking a few risks is just what I need.

CHAPTER 9

Brennan

I QUICKLY FINISH THE THREE PARLORS ASSIGNED TO me. Luckily, my last two were still clean since they weren't reserved on my shift. Now what? The main club is still occupied, so I can't get in there to start cleaning the equipment yet. Maybe I'll find Seth and see if he needs help cleaning his remaining rooms.

My intentions are good until I detour through the foyer to get to the other side of the club. I pass by a door that is cracked open enough that I can see inside.

I really should keep going, but my curiosity wins. I inch closer, careful not to be seen. I can clearly see Silas in the center of the room, his elite pupils giving him their undivided attention. They're in various states of dress—from leather to lingerie. The group seems to have paired off a man for each woman. I wonder if they're strangers to each other or if they came together. Either way, this is already the weirdest thing I've ever seen.

Silas is saying something about the bare hand being the simplest yet effective way to try stingy spanking for the first time. My ears perk up as I strain to hear every detail. My back is now to the door, so I can see anyone who happens to come down the corridor. Then I hear him introduce Tory. What? I turn back quickly to look into the club. I really should have just kept going and found Seth.

Tory appears out of nowhere, half naked, wearing barely there lingerie or whatever the fuck it is. A leather bra barely contains her fake tits, and I swear if she moves wrong, her vagina is going to fall out of that leather thong. She flips her hair in that way that annoys me so much and stands next to Silas. I hear him tell her to assume the position, and my throat tightens. It's like a train wreck. I can't look away. I continue to watch as he bends her over his knee. He rubs her ass in gentle circles while he says something to his captive audience. Only, now my ears have decided to stop working. They're clogged with my own monologue of regret and expletives. How could I have been so fucking stupid? He was just in my bed cuddling with me. Now he's fondling another woman's ass like he wasn't just trying to hint that he plans on having me. I've been on cloud nine this entire time like our time actually meant something. I can't even blame him. This has my stupidity written all over it.

"Brennan?" I hear Seth's voice, so I look up. Yeah, I've managed to fuck up the "not get caught" snooping too.

"Hey. There you are. I was just coming to find you," I fib. "I was going to see if you needed any help cleaning your rooms."

"What are you doing outside this door then?" He's not buying my act. "And why do you look so sad?"

I'm about to tell him that I'm fine when a petite blonde wearing a mini skirt and midriff comes to the door. "Excuse me," she apologizes. "I was told to close this door." We both nod as she closes it.

Great! I'm sure Silas now knows that I was snooping. Why else would I be standing outside the club's door instead of doing the job I'm being paid to do?

"I guess we were disrupting their class," I tell Seth.

"At least she didn't slam the door in our faces."

"I don't know what has affected that pretty smile of yours, but you know you can talk to me. Just like our talk earlier, I will never share anything you confide in me."

"I know. And I can't thank you enough. The same applies to you," I reply genuinely. I'm just not ready to discuss what I just saw or how it made me feel.

Silas was open about him teaching the class, so it would make sense that it involves a demonstration. So why does it bother me so much to see it? Is it because it's her and I know she's had sex with him? It makes me sick to my stomach to think about his hands caressing her ass like that. One thing is for certain. I could never do anything with him if that's the way things are between him and Tory. She's doing me a favor. Now, my virginity can remain intact. There is nothing else for me to ponder.

"Come on, girl. Let's grab dinner. They'll be in there for at least another hour or so. We can't finish our job until then, so let's go take a break."

"Sure. That sounds like a great idea. I'm actually starving," I admit. It takes all that I have to give him a small smile. Today is turning out to be so depressing. I just need to find something else to focus on—like photography. I'll start tomorrow morning.

Silas

I finish day one of the class. It's been so long since I've led one, but it helped to have such an enthusiastic group. They were very attentive and asked plenty of questions. I hadn't planned on using Tory for the demonstration, but some of the questions I received deemed it necessary. They needed to see my technique, how much pressure to apply, and how to alternate with sensual rubbing. I haven't spanked a woman in front of an audience since my BDSM club days. I rarely visit them now, other than to research what's popular and possibly to recruit new members to add to my growing waiting list.

Tory was beyond thrilled to participate since things didn't quite go well with her visiting Brennan's room. I still need to address that with her. I don't want my spanking her for a live demonstration to muddy the already clouded waters. I'm not rewarding her jealous behavior with attention from me. She has already crossed the line twice.

I dismiss the group and instruct them to grab a

binder on the way out the door to study for discussion tomorrow. Inside, they will find detailed information on impact play that is partly my interpretation and philosophy. I've put together the information they need, such as different types of devices used in spanking in relation to their level of sting or thud as well as other characteristics, aftercare, and more. I don't necessarily consider myself a dominant in the true sense, nor do I have submissives. I do, however, like control. I'm a kinky bastard, and I like certain aspects of the BDSM world without being fully submersed in it. Spanking is what I enjoy the most—leaving my mark.

Tory walks up to me as I'm about to leave. "Can we talk?"

"Get dressed and meet me in my room in a half an hour. We will talk there." The corners of her lips turn up in a smile. She obviously thinks she is getting her way even though this is not going to be the talk she wants. I need to create some distance between us. She has changed the rules of the game, and now we can no longer play.

"Absolutely," she agrees. "I'll see you there." She puts an extra strut in her step as she twists her ass away from me. She wants to give me a show, but I have something to do first before I meet with her and preferably get a drink.

I use my master key card to enter Brennan's cabin. I know I shouldn't be invading her personal space, but as this is my fourth time, it's sort of becoming a habit. Besides, I think my justification warrants this impromptu intrusion. Unknowingly, Seth brought it to my attention that she had been outside my class today—but for how long, I don't know. It does tell me that she is more curious than she lets on. By now, she and Seth should be busy putting the spanking toys and equipment away and cleaning the club. This is the perfect time to drop off one of the same binders that I gave my class to study. It's an opportunity to introduce her to my point of view on the subject in her own private time. If she is brave enough, she can follow up with questions if she wants. Last night when she was with her co-workers, I sensed unasked questions stirring in that pretty little head of hers.

I place the binder on her bed with another sticky note attached. This one simply says "Book of Knowledge." Can't wait for her vanilla perspective to be tainted with the thing that gets me off the most. Her response will determine how I proceed. I back out of her room, unfazed that I'm crossing the line once again.

The closer I get back to my room, the less I'm inclined to deal with Tory. Unfortunately for me, she is already waiting on my deck when I arrive. I opt to forgo that drink for now in order to expedite this discussion.

"There you are, handsome," she says excitedly when she sees me. She's wearing some bandage dress that fits her like a second skin. All the dresses she wears are skintight because she loves to flaunt her figure. I smile to myself because even with her overt sex appeal, I can't help but think about the sexy virgin who is the complete opposite.

"There it is. That's the smile I miss so much," she coos. If only she knew it wasn't for her.

"We need to talk, Tory," I begin. "Even though I don't want a relationship, you have been great. I'm so thankful for you, and I appreciate you stepping up to help with my class today."

"Yeah. I'm a visual learner myself, so anything to help. I mean absolutely anytime. You know I enjoy being spanked just as much as you enjoy spanking." She pushes off the rail to saunter up to me. "That reminds me," she adds while running her hands down my chest. I grab her by the wrists to stop her roaming hands.

"This is what I needed to talk with you about. I think we need to take a break."

"A break from what, Silas? You just said we weren't

in a relationship," she says, rolling her eyes. I know what she's doing. She's trying to bait me into warming her ass up with my belt for the blatant disrespect. "Expectations are changing. You want something I can't give you. Your jealous behavior is such a turn-off that I have to reconsider what we're doing."

"It's her, isn't it? That's why you're bringing up the jealousy thing. I'm not, by the way. That girl couldn't hold a candle to what I offer. My sex skills alone would run circles around her. Just be honest with me, Silas. You owe me that." She wiggles her wrist free. She doesn't question my presence in Brennan's room, but I can see it in her creased brows and sad eyes.

"What is it that you want to hear?" Damn, I should have had that drink. I'm not in the mood for one of her tantrums. The only reason I'm being tolerant is because this is my fault. I let things go too far and for too long. I should have changed shit up a long time ago before I even set eyes on Brennan. Time equates to developing feelings unless you have the apathy that I've acquired for love.

"The truth," she fumes. "You want to end this non-relationship affair with me so you can take a shot at Brennan. She has your attention now." Her voice cracks with that last accusation. She is not far from the truth. I need to end things with her because she is

116

becoming clingy, and I do potentially want to have my way with Brennan. I'm just not sure if it will ever come to pass.

"This is exactly why. You're proving my point and making this easy. If we've established that we were just fucking, then you have no right to question me. I don't ask you or care who you're fucking, and I expect the same in return."

She drops to her knees, and I'm caught off guard for a second. She pulls her dress beneath her tits to distract me as she reaches for the button of my jeans. She manages to get the button undone and is struggling with the zipper before I can grab her wrists again.

"Tory, stop!" I warn. Desperation is not a good look on her.

"Let me make you forget her—remind you how much you like it when I take you to the back of my throat," she pleads. Those words hit me with the force of bricks. My cock strains ever so slightly against my zipper because I know just how fucking good she is at giving head. I definitely don't need to be reminded because it's part of why I've kept her around this long. My brief hesitation is enough time for her to pull my jeans down to my ankles, albeit, I'm still wearing my boxer briefs. She licks her lips in appreciation when she sees my erection.

"See. Even your dick agrees with me. Let me make him happy."

I'm about to reiterate that we're done when an audible gasp pierces the air. We both turn to see a pale Brennan frozen in shock.

"Um, I'm so sorry," she apologizes profusely. She nearly trips as she runs away from us.

Fuck. This is not good. This is clearly not what it looks like, and I have a feeling I just took a million steps back with her. This is the absolute worst thing imaginable that could have happened. The misconception of what she just saw disturbs me more than it should, but I can't make myself to play it cool. I take one look at Tory's now smug face, and I lose it.

"Get the fuck out, Tory. We're done. Don't come up here again. Get back to keeping shit professional, or I will have to transfer you," I shout. Fuck the kid gloves. I'm pissed that I let things with her escalate once again. I don't know who I'm angrier with—her or myself. She knows not to push further. She stands to adjust her tits back into her dress before storming off. That fucking drink is long overdue. I need to find a way to fix this. If Brennan decides not to sleep with me, I want it to be on her own terms, not because she thinks something is still going on between Tory and me.

I've remained in my room since the whole incident with Tory today. I grab a pair of swim trunks to throw on because I need to get some laps in to clear my mind. I'm nearly to the bottom step when a familiar sound has me looking at the far end of the pool. Brennan slices through the water at blazing speed. It's a sight to watch as she changes from freestyle to the butterfly stroke. She looks like a mermaid because her hair is loose and flowing behind her. I hurry to stand at the end of the pool, but she simply flips underneath the water and heads in the opposite direction. I dive into the pool but am careful to stay out of her lane. I'll wait her out.

She finally tires and comes up on the other side. I waste no time swimming over to her. "That was pretty impressive. Where did you learn to swim like that?" I start with small talk to get a grasp on where her mind is after today. Did she get my binder? Well, of course, she did. The question is did she read it. Probably not.

"My mother," she replies. Two words are better than none, I guess.

"Well, the butterfly is the one stroke I struggle with because it combines the breaststroke with a dolphin kick. Too much work." I chuckle. "Maybe you can teach me how you do it."

"I'm sure you have enough money to hire someone way more qualified than I am to teach you," she chides. Yup. She is definitely upset about today—just as I thought.

"True, but what if I want you to teach me?"

"What do you want, Mr. Lair? I don't want to keep you from the laps that I'm sure you came down here to do." She isn't giving an inch. Just direct and cold. I know the answer to this suggestion before it leaves my mouth, but I try anyway.

"I was going to ask if you wanted to come upstairs with me and roast marshmallows over the fire pit under the moonlight."

"I don't think that is a good idea. I won't be making any more trips up there anyway. Thank you for the invitation, but I'm afraid I'm going to have to decline." She hurriedly gets out the pool to get away from me, and my chest tightens in defeat.

"It's not what you think, you know. Nothing happened between Tory and me. I was just telling her that things were over when you showed up. She pulled my pants down, but I wouldn't let her have me. I didn't touch her. I—" She cuts me off before I can finish explaining.

"With all due respect, sir, it's none of my business.

Please don't let yourself into my room again. I will return the binder you left in my room to your club tomorrow." She doesn't even give me the courtesy of a reply. I'm left watching that damn t-shirt she wears over her one piece cling to her body as she walks away. Why do I give a shit? I told her that I wouldn't chase her, but now my mind is even more unsettled than before. I have an overwhelming need to make things right.

I swim so many laps that I lose count. And still, thoughts of her muddle my mind. She has the upper hand right now, and the feeling is foreign as fuck. Things can't be left this way. I just need to find an opening back into her good graces, and fuck me, it can't have anything to do with sex. I climb out of the pool and rush to my room with renewed hope. I know exactly where to start.

CHAPTER 10

Silas

1 Week Later

I SWITCH IT UP TONIGHT WITH A GLASS OF WHISKEY before pulling out my cell phone. My fingers hoover over the keys in hesitation for a brief second before I compose my message to Brennan. I need to start just right, so she doesn't ignore me. I've allowed a week to pass. Hopefully, she'll be more receptive to converse with me.

Silas: *I was going through my things, and I came across my camera that I never use. I thought about you because it would be great for you to learn on. That is if you're interested in real photography.*

A few minutes past. Maybe she is in the shower and hasn't seen my message yet. I won't let myself think about the alternative—that she is ignoring me. Finally, after what seems like a lifetime, I see the three dots that lets me know she is responding.

Brennan: *Of course, I'm interested in real photography. I want to take the type of pictures my mother took, but I couldn't accept your camera. Thanks for offering.*

Silas: *Do you consider us friends? Forget about the Tory crap and ask yourself if you could see yourself building a friendship with me?*

I really have enjoyed her company. She is such a refreshing change. If things truly are impossible between us on a sexual level, I'd rather have her in my life as a friend than not at all. That's saying a lot, considering I don't have platonic relationships with the opposite sex. I only want to fuck them. Also, I know that friendship is the building block to more for someone like her. I will appeal to her sensibilities since she doesn't want what most women want from me—money and celebrity status.

Brennan: *Why would you want to be friends with*

me? We don't have anything in common. We're from two different worlds, where I don't fit in. I have nothing to offer that would add value or enrichment to your life.

That comment pisses me off, but I'll keep quiet about it for now. I hate that she thinks the rich are somehow better. I'm going to make it my personal mission to improve her self-esteem. She is simply stunning, and she doesn't even know it because she's allowing her lack of wealth to shape her worth. She's seen her mother work as "the help" her whole life, and now she's taken on that mentality. *Such bullshit.*

Silas: *It's exactly why I want to be friends. You're different, and I'm different when I'm around you. I don't want just another socialite around me, pretending to be my friend. It's oddly refreshing that you just see me— Silas or Mr. Smug Hottie—and not my money.*

I can't believe I just admitted all that, but it's the truth. Until now, I didn't know what her appeal to me was. I don't chase women. With any other woman, I would have already been on to the next. I even told her that I wouldn't chase her, yet I'm drawn to her, and I'm helpless to stop it. This scenario between us seems painfully familiar, but even so, I still can't just leave her alone.

Brennan: *Well, when you put it that way, how can I say no? Of course, I want to be your friend. I can't be*

more than that, but I think a friendship would be won-
derful. I'm different when I'm with you too.

To hear her admit she also acts different when
around me gives me even more hope. Not to get in her
pants, but to change her jaded view of the world. It's
not about who has the most money. We have the same
problems as anyone else, and sometimes more because
of what our status brings. Money equals expectations.

Silas: *Then it's settled. We're friends, and friends*
loan each other stuff. I'll let you borrow the camera, and
I'll even teach you how to use it.

Brennan: *Fine. You've twisted my arm. Seriously,*
thank you. I've taken some nice pics of things on the boat
with my phone, but I admit, it would be awesome to get
some better shots. I promise to take care of it.

Silas: *I'm sure you will. And you're welcome. I think*
you should start a portfolio so that you have a visual
medium to evaluate as your skills grow. Let's start with
capturing the sunrise in the morning. You can meet me
where we first met around 6am. That'll give you a half-
hour to familiarize yourself with the camera's features
before the sun actually rises.

I'm waiting for her to shoot down the idea since
she said that she wouldn't be coming back to my space
when we were at the pool. I could have suggested that
we meet on the fourth floor of the aft since that's where

the outdoor pool is, and it's open to everyone. The thing is, I need her back in my personal space. I need to know that we've somewhat resolved her issue with me, and this is the best way I can think of. Fuck neutral territory; I need her on mine. I'm not giving up the chance for more; I just need to slow things down a bit and appeal to what she wants. It will have to be her decision.

Brennan: *That's really early, but I'll be there. I can't wait to see the difference in the pictures. I've never had a real camera before. I looked up the cost of some on the phone you gave me, and let's just say without you loaning yours, it was out of the question. Thank you again.*

Score one for me. She's accepted my invitation to meet me on my turf. The camera idea was genius. The crazy thing is, it's not some ploy to get in her pants. It makes me happy to know that my small act of kindness will mean everything to her. Having her in my company again is the bonus. I sip the last of my whiskey, finally content.

Silas: *Get some rest then, buttercup. See you bright and early. Don't be late. I can't wait to see the pictures you capture and watch as your ability grows. Night :)*

Brennan: *Night, Silas. I won't be late.*

My alarm sounds at a quarter to five, and it feels like I just closed my eyes. I throw on a pair of jeans, wash my face, and brush my teeth. The time is creeping by. I pass the rest of the time until Brennan's arrival by ordering a huge breakfast for us. I don't know what she likes, so I just get some of everything. The food actually arrives before she does but only by a few minutes.

I left my level open to below, so I can sit in the shadows and watch her approach like a creeper. Holy hell, she's actually wearing a dress—and even more surprisingly, it fits. Not in the obscene way that Tory wears her dresses, but a relaxed fit t-shirt dress that just brushes her knees. It's simple yet sexy. That's her, though. Understated sexy. I see her looking around the deck for me. She's never actually been inside my lair. I slide the glass door back and watch as she takes me in. She peruses my body slowly since I deliberately didn't put on a shirt. I never said I would not try to win her over. And from the eye fuck she just gave me, she likes what she sees. I step back and let her in, playing oblivious to what I just noticed.

"I took the liberty of ordering breakfast for us again. I don't know what you like, so I got some of everything," I say.

"Thank you. I'm actually starving since I had an early dinner last night."

"Well, let's get you fed."

She is looking around my space now, so she is a bit caught off guard when I grab her hand to lead her to my dining table. She flinches at first, but then her fingers intertwine with mine. Her petite feminine hand feels like it was meant to fit in mine. I pull out her chair while holding her until the last possible second. What the hell is wrong with me? *It's because of the chase*, I tell myself.

"You have a lovely suite," she says, continuing to look around.

"Would you like a tour?"

"Maybe another time. I don't want to miss the sunrise."

That's right. How quickly did I forget the point of her visit at this hour.

"Right! Here. What do you like?" I ask as I begin to add pancakes to her plate. "Sausage?" She just chuckles and nods to all my offerings. By the time I finish, her plate is beyond full.

"You are not going to eat all that," I tease.

"Why? Because it will all go to my ass?" Her infectious smile wavers, and I could kick someone for making her self-conscious about her body.

"Your ass is perfect, so don't ever let anyone tell you differently," I chastise. "I meant there was no way your tiny self could put away that much food, so I'm volunteering to help."

Before she could let my intent sink in, I straddle her lap and cut a bite-size piece of pancake with my fork. I drown it with maple syrup and edge it slowly toward her lips. Yes, I'm abandoning my ease back into her good graces strategy. I will follow her cues of what she lets me slide with. It's hard to stick to a plan of slow when I'm with her.

"Open," I command softly. She surprises me by obeying. Our proximity is so intimate, and then I just upped it a notch by feeding her. Holy shit! Watching her take a bite is so damn erotic. She licks the residual syrup from her lips, and I don't know how long I can keep this from escalating to more. I don't want to ruin our miraculous progress.

"Your turn," she insists. I take another bite-size piece with the same fork ready to place my lips where hers just were. Only she surprises me yet again by taking the fork out of my hand. "Turnabout is fair play, Mr. Lair," she whispers before feeding me the bite. My dick strains against my jeans, and my chest heaves. I've never been so turned on by something as innocent as this—this vanilla.

There is so much I can say right now. God knows the lewd thoughts that are wreaking havoc on my mind, but I don't want to push too hard. Whether she knows it or not, we're establishing a mental game of foreplay that will end with her underneath me. There's no denying how much she wants me too. Her eyes give her away. She's just rebelling against what her body craves because she's scared. Good thing I have time. We go back and forth, feeding each other everything on the plate until we both notice the beginning of the sunrise.

"I'll grab the camera," I say as I dab the bacon grease from the side of her mouth. I can't resist giving her a wink as I do so, and it earns me another smile. I reluctantly get up to grab the camera from my bed where I left it this morning. When I get back, she is already out on the deck, looking toward the sky.

She turns to watch me as I walk out to meet her. Her eyes are giving her away again, and it gives me an idea. I hand her the camera bag, and she wastes no time looking through it. She pushes a strand of hair back that escaped from that bun hairdo she wears. Her hair is too pretty for that shit. I just want to pull all the pins out. My fingers are twitching to do just that. She puffs out a breath of frustration as she fiddles with the camera. She's getting overwhelmed with it all.

"Hey. Let's just get you some practice shots in. Point and shoot. Then later you can read the instruction manual and learn about all the features and how to work them all," I suggest as I steady her hands in mine.

She finally nods and aims the camera toward the sunrise. She takes a few shots before we look at them together on the LCD display.

"See? Not bad. Not bad at all for your first time. Those are actually pretty good."

"Oh, it's definitely your camera. I can't take that much credit. What kind of camera is this?"

"Nikon D800," I say, pointing at the name on the camera. We both laugh, but then she points the camera at me. "What do you think you're doing?"

"I want to shoot you. I mean take your picture. You know what I mean," she corrects.

"I'm not a fan of having my picture taken, but for you, I guess it'll be okay," I reply, only somewhat teasing. "I'll be your subject. How do you want me to pose?"

"Do whatever you want. I just want to try something."

I grab the rail and face her so that all my tattoos are in her line of sight. She snaps quite a bit before she finally lowers the camera.

"Okay, let's see." We look at the LCD display again, and I'm amazed at what she was able to capture. "Wow.

Good job!"

"You're kind of beautiful," she confesses. She blushes when she realizes that she said that out loud. I miss that lovely shade on her even though it would be nicer somewhere else—like on her ass.

"Right back atcha, doll. Glad you think so."

"Um, so how do I get the pics?" Her attempt to change the subject is endearing, but I let her get away with it.

"There's a memory card inside so we can download them to a computer, or once we stop at the first port, we can find a place to print them."

"Okay," she agrees.

I grab the camera and point it at her. "What are you doing?" She covers her face with her hands.

"Turnabout is fair play. Remember, Miss Delavan?" I use one hand to lower her guarded hands, and she lets me. Then I do something I've been dying to do. I pull those stupid pins out of her hair until her raven locks tumble free. She shakes her head and runs her fingers through the waist-length tresses as I snap away. She blows a shy kiss to the camera, and something comes over me. I wrap the strap around my neck, rotate the camera behind me, and pull her into my arms.

Her breath hitches, but she doesn't pull away. I

throw caution to the wind and lean in further. We're both on the precipice of something bigger than us. I capture her lips in mine, and this time, she doesn't hesitate to open to me. I deepen the kiss as her hands roam my chest then down to my stomach. She moans into my mouth, and it takes the strength of a saint not to take her to my bed and fuck her right now.

I'm into some twisted shit, so slow is key. This is the first step toward us being more than just the "friends" that I proposed. I'm still opposed to a relationship, but I want her. I can't wait to feel my cock slide in and out of her tightness.

Reluctantly, I'm the one to break the kiss this time. Only because I know where this heading if I don't pump the brakes.

"I have an early class this morning, love. I need to get some prep work in before then." She rubs her lips and looks away from me.

"Oh, okay." I don't want her to get the wrong idea. That fucking kiss was scale shattering hot.

"You're welcome to stay and have some more of that breakfast we didn't finish if you want," I add. I remove the camera from around my neck and place it around hers.

"No. I'm going to head back to my room. Thank you for breakfast and for letting me use your camera."

She tries to hand it back to me, but I refuse.

"Hold on to it. I want you to go learn about the different features. Then you can teach me," I reply with a wink.

"I doubt I could teach you anything, but I'll accept that challenge."

"Great. Let's plan on having our nightly swim tonight, but bring the memory card from the camera. We can download the pictures to my laptop afterward."

"Deal!" She half jumps from excitement. That's the response I was going for.

"See you later, beautiful." That enticing shade of red disappears inside her dress, and I can't wait to make her blush naked so I can see. Yeah. Today was a success.

"Later," she bids. There is an extra bounce in her step as she leaves the way she came. Wait until she's had my cock. I want to see her walk then. It's only a matter of time now.

CHAPTER 11

Brennan

I'VE REPLAYED MY TIME WITH SILAS THIS MORNING on a constant loop today. His flirtatious gestures never faltered, and an added sweetness has me thinking about him differently. His offer to loan me his camera so I could learn photography changed my mind about giving him a chance. I may have stared at the pics I took of him all through my shift. The camera definitely loves him. His blue eyes are hypnotic. I want him to look at me the way he did in those pictures while he eradicates my virtue. He makes me crave things I've never even thought about before. Like how would it feel to have my legs wrapped around him while he buries himself deep inside these walls. I know all the reasons we shouldn't get involved with one another, but I find myself wanting to take the leap anyway. I actually believe his explanation for what I saw with Tory. If the pushy, conniving demeanor from her little visit to warn me away from him is any indication, I'd say she was trying to use oral sex to get her way.

Their history is none of my business, and I don't want to be the timid girl who constantly gets pushed aside. Silas awakens a fire within me with a single touch, and I want to explore that. If he's willing to leave Tory alone, then I'm willing to jump. Jump into exploring whatever this chemistry is that burns between us. I'm not looking for anything more than that. It's time I finally embrace my sexuality, and I want to start with him.

I've waged an exhausting war with myself this past week on whether to go through with my plan. Seduction wins the battle over continuing to let the chips fall where they may. I used my debit card for the first time in forever to purchase a pink bikini from the gift shop today. No oversized t-shirts covering my one piece tonight. I need Silas to see me as sexy and desirable. I wish I had more experience in the flirting department, but hey, how hard can it be? I spend extra time shaving every inch of myself with the razors I bought at the same little gift shop. I pay special attention to my lady parts. Normally, she gets just a little trim, but tonight she gets the bald treatment. I'm not satisfied until I'm smooth all over. When I step out of the shower, I do a little twirl in front of the floor-length mirror behind the door. I want to see what he will see, but I allow a hint of doubt to creep through my fading confidence at the imperfections in my reflection. Hoping for a toner body or the disappearance of the stretch marks on my ass won't do me any good, so I quickly wrap myself in a towel. Maybe I can insist he leaves the light off. We only need to feel anyway.

The notification ping of my phone has me nearly jumping out of my skin. The pep talk I'm having with myself will have to wait. I rush to my bed to retrieve my phone, knowing it can only be one person. Time is up. Either I push forward with this plan to finally have Silas, or I chicken out like a virginal coward. I use my thumbprint to unlock my phone—allowing procrastination to let the decision linger.

Silas: *Are you ready for that swim?*

I'm amazed that it is already after eight p.m.

Amazed at how long getting ready took for me to feel fuckable.

Me: *Yes. I was doing some light reading until I heard from you.*

Silas: *Light reading, huh? Was it by any chance the binder I left for you?*

Until now, we've both opted not to bring up the ass spanking book. Our flirtations were strained a bit after the incident with Tory, and although I never took the binder back to him the next day, we both took a minuscule step back. I can't speak for him, but I needed to re-evaluate how I would proceed with him. I'll never be willing to be someone's option. If Tory is who he wanted, then that meant there was no room for me. His explanation of the event seemed likely, but his tenderness this morning is what I needed. I don't need the fairy tale or the happily ever after; I just want to let go for once. I want to have amazing sex with this hot guy and savor the memories.

Silas: *Are you still there?*

My phone pings again, and I realize I never answered him.

Me: *Yes, I'm here. No, I haven't had a chance to wade through the ass porn you left for me.*

Silas: *Ass porn? You kill me with the words you put together. Meet me at our spot in 10 and don't forget that* *memory card.*

He didn't elaborate on the binder, and I'm thankful. That thing is a whole other can of worms. Baby steps. One thing at a time. I'd be lying if I said I haven't taken an itsy-bitsy peek and found myself more than slightly intrigued. Mostly because it was an intimate look at his mind—his world.

Me: *See you in 10*

I snatch the pink bikini dangling from the armoire and rid it of the price tag. The decision has been made. Like a fork in the road, the bikini represents letting myself enjoy one memorable night with him while the old one piece represents status quo. I slide the barely there fabric onto my body. The halter top pushes my breasts up and together for never-ending cleavage, and I struggle to keep my ass from swallowing up the bottoms. Maybe I should have tried this on before buying. I'm sure this is the way it's supposed to fit, but I just feel so exposed. My flaws have nowhere to hide. At the last minute, I slide my trusty oversized t-shirt over the bikini before heading out of the door. *Baby steps.*

Silas is already in the pool swimming laps when I arrive. Just as he flips against the pool edge to head back in my direction, I know I only have seconds to muster the confidence I found earlier. He hasn't seen me yet. Without hesitation or further thought, I pull the t-shirt off. I'll just fake it for now. The shirt catches on my bun, unraveling it with my constant pull to get the shirt off. When I manage to stop fussing with the shirt, I see that Silas has not only made it back to this end, but that he's also witnessed the entire spectacle. His grin tells me he saw it all. My first attempt at seduction is a hot mess right from the start. I should just give up before I make too big of a fool of myself if that's possible.

He uses the edge of the pool to boost himself out the water, providing a distraction from my own clumsiness. Water drips down his body as he runs his hand through his hair. Every defined muscle begs for my fingers to touch them. The bulge restrained behind those swim trunks begs to be freed and licked. He strolls over to me, and I don't know where to put my hands. I think about my hips, but that just seems too obvious. I feel awkward as if I'm already trying too hard.

"Nice suit," Silas says, breaking through my internal meltdown. He walks a circle around me, making no attempt to hide that he is checking me out. And what do I do? I just stand here like an out of my league idiot, waiting for him to judge me. I know my body is a far cry from Tory's.

"Figured it was time for a new one." I try to fill the

air with useless chatter, wanting him to stop looking so hard.

"If you're going to show this much skin, sweetheart, you have to own it."

"It's just a swimsuit, Silas. I'm sure you've seen women in less." I'm not fooling him one bit. I'm sure my insecurities radiate from me.

"Hmmm, maybe so. None worn quite like this, though."

He slips a finger between the tie at my hip. One pull and my bottoms would fall off. I don't move his hand, though. I don't speak a fucking word. Let him do it. Make my mission easier by doing all the work himself. He's a breath away from me now, and I can feel his body heat intertwining with mine. A look passes between us of unspoken promises. He removes his finger, and I immediately feel bereft. Is that it? Damn him. I just need to work harder to show him I'm willing.

"Why don't we skip the swim for now? Let's head up to my place," he suggests. Now, he's talking. I nod, and he leads the way. When we reach the top level, the ambiance is already set. The fire pit is blazing, casting light on what looks like strawberries and champagne on ice. Orange pillows surround the flame. Mr. Lair appears to have his own plan of seduction waiting, and dammit to hell, it's better than mine is.

"What's all this?" I ask nonchalantly. "You have a hot date coming after I leave?"

He laughs, and the tone stirs up butterflies in my belly—or is it my nerves?

"Very cute, Brennan. Just thought you'd appreciate a little something different tonight besides my Macallan. You seem like a champagne kind of woman."

"Ah, I see. And the strawberries?" I'll play along with his little game.

"Strawberries enrich the flavor of the champagne, of course. Can't have one without the other." He takes a seat on one of the stuffed pillows and pulls me down next to him before pouring me a glass.

"But of course."

He is too funny when he's like this. Those dimples and cleft chin make me melt just a little bit more. The flames dance in those mischievous eyes of his as they darken with promise. Surprisingly, after getting a firsthand look at my imperfections, he still seems interested.

"What kind of champagne is this?" I ask, actually appreciating the flavor. The rose-colored bottle is pretty too. Definitely better than the scotch that cost more than a home. Just thinking about it is insane.

"Armand de Brignac Brut Rose Champagne."

"You want to try that again in English?" I tease.

"That's a mouthful."

"Not yet." He winks.

I don't miss that ginormous innuendo. That fucker has flashing lights around it. I take a huge gulp of my "whatever the hell he called it" champagne—lost for the right comeback. "Not another half a mil?" I ask. I'm stepping right over that last comment for now.

"No. Significantly less at ten grand, but that's not what I'm thinking about." Holy shit, that's still a lot of money, but I indulge where he's going with this.

"So *what* are you thinking about?"

"Sure you want to know, buttercup? You can't unask the question, so make sure you're ready to hear what plagues my mind."

He takes slow but steady sips of the champagne he just poured for himself. He is giving me an out, a chance to turn this bullet train around, but I'm not going to take it.

"Keep moving like a bullet train." I quote the lyrics from the song "Bullet Train" by Stephen Swartz featuring Joni Fatora. His dimples make their reappearance as he understands what I'm saying. It's one of the songs he added to my phone. I'm giving him the green light without having to actually come out and say it.

"Yeah?" he questions. I nod. "I'd rather show you."

He knocks back the remaining contents of his

champagne glass before getting up and disappearing. *What the hell?* Then I hear it. It's the song. *Moving like the speed of sound.* It plays in surround sound, filtering around the deck. He returns and takes his seat back on the pillow.

He picks up a single strawberry and rubs it across my lips until I take a bite. He takes the next bite. We go back and forth like this, eating a few of them before he gets bolder. He trails one down my breast in the shape of an "S." He then licks the path that he just drew with the strawberry. His tongue along my heated skin makes me shiver. He takes another strawberry from the bed of ice and leans me back. My breath catches in my throat as he traces another path, lower than the one before, and my vagina throbs the minute his tongue strokes my flesh. My hands grab a fist full of his hair on their own, and that's the only encouragement he needs. He unties my bikini bottoms with only two pulls. The only thing keeping them up is the fact that I'm still sitting on the fabric. *Well, I was.*

Crouching before me, he lifts my legs up and over his shoulders before I can even blink. Holy hell, he's strong. My bottoms fall away, and my bare pussy is lined up with his mouth. I fall back against the pillow, ready for him to take me in his mouth, but there is a pause.

"You're going to watch every second of me devouring this sweet pussy. I want you to see how greedy my tongue is for you right now."

"Yes." I don't even know what the hell I'm saying. He didn't ask me a question. He was giving me instructions he intends for me to follow.

The first lick to my clit has me buckling before he even gets into it. The sensation isn't like anything I've ever felt. I wasn't ready. He tightens his grip on my thighs, and this time, he latches onto my nub.

"Ahhhh," I cry out. He begins a skillful tempo of licks and nibbles. The tremor of my legs is uncontrollable. I can't reach his hair now, and I need something to hold. He swirls his tongue around my clit once more before he explores my depths. Every plunge of his wicked tongue inside me makes it impossible to focus. His back flexes beneath my calves as he pushes further inside. I can no longer hold on. My head falls back while my body writhes from his oral assault. His mouth is insanely talented, and all I can do is ride the wave of my first orgasm as he rips it from me.

"Silas … shit!" I moan his name like a woman possessed. He doesn't stop. He sucks every last drop until a second orgasm rolls into the first one. Euphoria takes over, and I feel like I'm falling. It's all too much. Suddenly, something cold drizzles down my folds.

It's the damn champagne. The coldness revs up the dissipating ache—snowballing into a sensation that can't easily be put into words. He sucks my champagne-laced juices with fervor and stars explode behind my eyes when yet another orgasm chases down the first two.

"This is how I like my champagne. That's what I was thinking about. I bought it with you in mind," he confesses before licking through my aftershocks.

He eases my legs down, but I swear I can't move. I just had three amazingly perfect orgasms. I've gotten myself off before, but what he just accomplished doesn't even compare. That was another level of coming that I've been missing out on until now.

"So would you like some more champagne?" he asks like he didn't just have my pussy in his mouth. Like he didn't just shatter my world with his tongue. I nod, so he pours me another glass. I sure as hell need it after that. "Guess I've found something else that enriches the taste of the champagne besides strawberries."

And just like that, my vag aches for another go. I'm ready to see what other tricks he has in his arsenal. I stare at his lips with a newfound appreciation.

"Keep staring at me like that, Brennan, and you're going to get fucked."

"Maybe that's what I'm hoping for," I admit

brazenly. I surprise myself. Not Silas, though. It's like he knew it all along.

"Tasting your cunt was something I could no longer stave off. I've thought about it all day. Don't tempt me with the pleasure of being your first unless you're absolutely sure. I can't offer you anything but the promise to fuck you to a plethora of earth-shattering orgasms. No relationship and no commitments."

I note his warning, and it's as I expected. I don't want anything from him but that tongue again and his cock. I had known this before I agreed to come up here.

"Do you always try to talk women out of having sex with you?" I playfully roll my eyes to lighten the now heavier mood. "I'm absolutely sure, and you can trust that I don't want anything other than what you just promised."

"Well, in that case, doll, let's take this inside. Your first time is not going to be on pillows on the ground. I'm not that much of an asshole." He smirks.

I'm taking that leap, and I'm not looking back. I wanted this, and now, I will have him—even if it is just for tonight. It's my decision.

CHAPTER 12

Silas

S HE WAITS FOR ME TO GET UP FIRST. I ENJOY THE show of her failing miserably to hide her pussy from me with those bikini bottoms. The strings dangle against her leg as the thin material does nothing for her efforts.

"You really want to cover up now after I've been tongue deep within your sacred walls? I've already committed your sweetness to memory," I point out. "Now to leave a lasting impression of my cock deeper than any man will ever go."

"Well, aren't you modest?" she quips.

"Just being forthcoming, love. I'm going to depths that will be unreachable for years to come."

I'm blessed with anatomy that men would shed a tear for. I don't like to brag on my dick because the minute it's freed, it is its own warning label. I only speak of it now because her first time with me is going to set the bar. Any man who's lucky enought to be with her after me will most likely be a massive disappointment.

"We shall see," she challenges as if I could possibly be mistaken.

"That's it," I growl. I rush her before she has a chance to react. I pick her up and throw her over my shoulder while simultaneously snatching away those cock tease bottoms of hers.

I enter my domain all caveman like and plop her sexy ass onto my bed.

"Real smooth there, stud." She fake pouts, but I don't miss her brisk movements to cover her body with my sheets.

Her bashfulness at this moment is a testament to her inexperience. She deserves nothing less than a memorable night. I've decided to change gears.

"Turn over on your stomach," I tell her. The moonlight filters through my floor-to-ceiling windows, but it's enough to see her apprehension. I crawl onto the bed with her, helping her do as I have asked.

"What are you going to do? I can't see if I'm on my stomach," she whines.

I swear this is the most patient I've ever been with a woman. These questions simply don't exist when it's time to fuck. They can't get their clothes off fast enough. She's worth it, though.

"You don't need to see, only feel. Now, turn over so I can give you a back massage." I give her ass a testing slap, and she flinches in surprise. She didn't cry out in pain or protest, so that fuels my curiosity of how far I can take her. Would she enjoy it? She doesn't say anything else, so I guide her hips until she is on her stomach.

I lean over to my nightstand and grab my remote and rose body oil out of the drawer. With a single click, we are showered in light.

"Oh, no, Silas. Please, no lights." The distinctive tremble of her voice clues me in to her nervousness. She's back lying on her side in a flash. Yes, she's a virgin, but it's not that. She's not here with me at the moment. Something else is causing her insecurities. This won't suffice.

"I'm not going to fuck you in the dark, Brennan."

"I thought you said you don't need to see, only

feel?" she says, giving my words right back to me. I'm not budging on this.

"Not the same, sweetheart. There's one thing I won't budge on, and that's when you cross the threshold of my domain, I'm the boss, and I make the rules. There's no way I'm going to pass on seeing your pussy up close and personal in the light or the sex faces you make when I bring you to orgasm after orgasm."

"But you're already the boss outside your domain, and you make the rules out there too."

I sense a hint of sarcasm as she tries not to laugh. I can't help it. I fall next to her and laugh my ass off. Nobody would dare stand up to me this way right before sex, and I kind of like it.

"I think you are begging for me to spank your ass," I accuse.

Then suddenly shit gets serious. "Fine. Just look at all my stretch marks up close and personal with your *boss* light on," she chides.

She tries to say it jokingly; only, I see the truth not far from the surface. Her nervousness is because she is self-conscious about her body? *What the actual fuck?* Is she really making a big deal over the one stretch mark on her ass? I have no words to that insanity. Instead, I convey my disagreement in the best way possible. I lean down and run my tongue along the imperfection that is causing a strain on the mood. I kiss and caress it, giving it the attention it should have. It's part of her, so it's beautiful.

"You mean this single mark? Not plural, buttercup."

"Whatever. It's a bunch of littles ones buried deep within the one big one."

"Let's name them then." I can't conceal my mischievous grin.

"You want to name my stretch marks?" she asks in astonishment.

"Yup. That way you will understand it's a part of you, and therefore, it's beautiful. You can be on a first-name basis with them and accept them in your life."

"I can't believe we're having an entire conversation over my stretch marks. This is so sexy—such a mood killer."

"Exactly. Now embrace that it, as in singular, exists, and let's get back to where we were." My point has been made. I hope she sees how silly she was being.

"What should we call it?" she asks, ready to do as I've asked.

"Mine."

The minute that "off-limits" word leave my mouth, we both fall speechless. Why in the hell did I just say that? I don't do "mine."

"Stay right there."

I get up to grab the champagne and strawberries from outside to recreate the mood. But I also needed the breather because I can't have that kind of slip-up again. No pussy is that good. When I return, she is sitting cross-legged on my bed with my sheet draped across her. I see her pink bikini lying in a heap on the floor. I place the champagne and strawberries on the nightstand. She surprises me by turning over and lying flat on her stomach without me having to ask her again. I move aside the remaining sheet that has already begun to fall away. "Bullet Train" continues to play on a loop in the background, but neither of us minds it. I climb on to the bed and straddle her thighs before drizzling the rose-infused oil from her shoulders to her tailbone. The oil is a staple in my aftercare from playtime. Tonight, though, it serves as a sensual introduction for a memorable night to come.

I knead her back with moderate yet purposeful movement. Her feminine flesh beneath my hands stirs up an ache deep in my balls. I want to be massaging something else. Slow and steady is on the agenda, so I'm perfecting this newfound patience I have acquired.

"Hmmm, that feels good," she says approvingly. "Never had a massage before."

I'm beginning to question if she's experienced any

of life's little treasures. Better for me, actually, since I get to be the one she experiences it all with. She simply is exquisite. My hands slowly caress her sides until I come to the cute fucking dimples just above her perfectly heart-shaped ass. Other than that one stretch mark she is obsessed with, her pale skin is smooth, kissably soft, and flawless. Her heart-shaped face is naturally breathtaking without the enhancement of makeup. She reminds me of the old Jennifer Love Hewitt that guys would secretly jack their dicks to during puberty. Jennifer was a little before my time, but her old shows never grew old. In comparison, Brennan edges up the hotness factor by leaps and bounds.

It's nice to just massage and admire her body, but my dick wants to come out to play. It didn't get the patience via slow and steady memo. Besides, she is really relaxing. It would be a shame if I massaged her to sleep because then I would have to think of creative ways to wake her up. That could be promising too, but alas, I will move things along. I slide my hand down her back once more before letting it continue down the crack of her ass. Oh, the fun I plan on having with this ass. Maybe not tonight, but soon.

As I begin to rub her pussy, her legs spread in invitation. Her tight little cunt is hot and dripping with her essence. I use her juices to coat my fingers and make slow, deliberate circles. Alternating petting and massaging, I part her folds and introduce a finger. Just the tip. Her greedy pussy clenches around my finger as a moan escapes her.

"Does that feel good, doll?" She nods, but I want to hear her say it. I want the words to spill intelligibly from those lips.

"I can't hear you, Brennan. Answer me, or I will stop."

"Yee ... eee ... sss!" Exactly what I thought. She is so close. Can't have her coming just yet, though. I want to be balls deep for her first penetrative orgasm. My fingers just won't do. I slide my finger out of her heat, and without warning, I bring it to her mouth. I nudge her lips apart for her to suck.

"See how good you fucking taste? Your pussy is so wet right now. I can tell how badly you want to fuck me," I state. "You've been holding back, letting me think I was the only one who wanted this."

"I doooooo," she murmurs around my finger. She sucks with just the right amount of suction and pull. I imagine her lips wrapped around my dick instead. Straining against my semi still wet trunks now, it's begging to be let out of its containment. This has been an ongoing thing around her.

I love her like this. Guard down and at my mercy.

"Do what?" I ask, forcing her to elaborate.

"See how good I taste. But I bet you taste even better." My finger pauses in her mouth. She just hinted that she wanted to suck my dick. All blood drains to my shaft, not a coherent thought left. I need to be in her mouth now.

"So you're telling me that you want my cock in that fuckable mouth of yours?" I clarify.

"Turnabout is fair play," she reminds me, and it must be the sexiest fucking thing I've heard to date. Even though she's said it before, it wasn't in relation to sucking my dick. I pull my finger from her mouth and inch off the bed to remove my trunks.

"Let me," she insists, now sitting up on the bed once more.

Her skin glistens from the oil, and I'm mesmerized by the entire sight of her. She no longer wrestles with the cover to hide, so I'm guessing the champagne has relaxed some of her inhibitions. She scoots to the edge of the bed and grabs the side of my trunks. She slowly eases them down like she is revealing her prize. My dick finally springs free and bobbles as it jumps with excitement. While I kick my trunks the rest of the way off, she just stares, cataloging every detail of my length and thickness. I let her get a good look. I wish I knew the lewd thoughts that were running wild in her mind right now. She licks her pale pink lips in appreciation, and her eyes darken with brazen need. I warned her that my package was extensive and the depths that I plan to conquer.

Undiscouraged, she grabs my length. She takes a few introductory licks, getting acquainted with my size. Licking from base to tip, she explores the veins that provide a roadmap to my sensitive spots. When she finally opens wide enough to take me into her mouth, I swear I would shoot a load down her throat right then. My cock twitches against her tongue. She hollows her cheeks to take more of me, her suction perfect. I have to set the pace, or her hot little mouth is going to make me come before I'm ready.

I ease out of her mouth before slowly giving her a little more of my length. I'm careful not to take her too fast as we establish a comfortable rhythm.

"Your mouth is incredible. Absolutely, indisputably incredible."

This spurs her on. She tries to take more of me as she jacks my dick with the rest she can't fit into her mouth. I have other plans, though. I allow myself a few more enjoyable sucks before I pull completely out. Without instruction, I push her back on the bed and drop to my knees. My tongue plunges into her engorged, still dripping pussy with expert precision. I suck, nibble, and playfully bite her clit. I lean her back even further to give it a slight slap, and she buckles. This is the second time I've seen that telling response when applying a little pain. I need to explore that later. I return my assault to her honey spot, driving her to the orgasm I know is so close. Her legs tighten around my head, and she gets a fist of my hair.

"That's right, baby. Hold on for the ride," I encourage between licks.

I plunge my tongue deep into her opening as my other hand finds that bundle of nerves. I'm not going to even dwell on the fact that I just called her the one pet name I despise the most—baby. The grip she has on my hair and neck makes me desperate to see her come again—only this time in the light.

"Silas," she cries as she gives me what I've been waiting for. I watch her face as I continue to suck on her pussy through her aftershocks. And damn, does she come beautifully. The sex face she makes is worth the delayed gratification I'm imposing on myself.

CHAPTER 13

Brennan

SILAS PULLS ME TO STRADDLE HIS LAP AFTER giving me yet another mind-blowing orgasm with his sinful tongue. He leans back against the padded leather headboard while grabbing a single plump strawberry from the chilled bowl at his bedside.

"Open," he instructs with a gravelly tone that permeates through me, causing me to shudder.

His dominance should offend me as his directness doesn't leave room for hesitation or thought. The manner in which he transitions from playfulness to hot Dom guy excites me a bit more than it should. I do as I'm told as I focus my attention on his lips that were just acquainted with the most intimate parts of me. The softness of them is a stark contrast to his brown mustache that has hints of blond.

Being this close and personal—detailing his angular, chiseled face, dimples, and blue eyes—awakens the butterflies in my belly. My heart slams against my chest at just how damn pretty he is. And oddly enough, he wants me. His dick is mere inches from my throbbing pussy, yet he feeds me strawberries like he didn't just deliver an earth-shattering orgasm a few minutes ago. He leans over again, this time to pour me a glass of more champagne. He doesn't have to instruct me anymore to let him feed me. It's becoming our thing, and I have to say I like it. I'm not even fretting over being naked with him, but that's in part to the alcohol, I'm sure. I just want more kisses from him, so I boldly take them.

I drink the last of the champagne in my flute before leaning over him to put it back on the nightstand. My breast grazes his mouth as I do so, and he sticks his tongue out for a quick lick. I pull back just slightly so I can grab both sides of his head. I hold him still as I find his mouth with mine. He isn't expecting that.

A slow grin spreads before he gives in to my pursuit. I kiss him with the intensity building within me, this desperate need to consume him. I inch closer until I'm hovering over his cock. I rub myself against it, feeling the ache grow into an inferno of need ... feeling him lengthen and harden between us. I gyrate my hips, wanting to feel his thickness penetrate me. I'm ready. I've never been more sure of something in my life.

"Slow down there, cowgirl. Your next orgasm will be on my dick but inside your walls. I want that excited little pussy riding me just like that."

He slaps my ass, and the sting leaves even more wetness in its wake.

"I'm ready, Silas," I plead. He's got me all worked up. I'm ready for him to give me what he's been promising me all night. I'm ready for him to fuck me.

"Are you now?" That damn eyebrow of his arches up in the way he does that is too sexy to be fair. "I think the wetness gave that away, sweetness."

"Why are you teasing me? I thought you—"

I don't get to finish that question. He flips us over, and now he's hovering on top of me. He wraps my legs firmly around his hips as he pauses to slide a condom over his substantial cock. Holy shit, this is really happening. Will he fit? His eyes are trained on mine as he makes a show of sheathing himself. He strokes it a few times, and I find it pleasantly erotic. He lines his dick up at my entrance and slides it through my wetness, building me up more.

"Relax, sweetheart. Just feel."

I feel the pinch and then the burn. He stills briefly before introducing more of his cock. He stretches me open, and I welcome the bite of pain. Every inch he pushes in burns in an oddly delicious way. He continues his unhurried thrusts until I'm full of him. I throb around him. Pain and pleasure mix in a euphoric bliss. Just as the pain begins to dissipate, he begins to move.

"Shit!" I cry out, but he doesn't stop.

Those captivating blues pin me to the bed as he begins a leisurely stroke. The pain intensifies until all that remains is the stars dancing behind my eyes. Stars I have come to welcome. My hips begin to move on their own accord, desperate for every inch he's keeping away from me. I want them all. Sensing my need, he drives deeper.

"This pussy was made for me. I can tell by how tight it clenches for me. Feels so fucking incredible."

His eyes never leave mine as he picks up the pace. The sound of his balls slapping against my wetness echoes through his suite. He pulls me tighter as his hips begin to piston harder—deeper.

"Ahhhh," I scream out.

"Am I hurting you, love? Is it too much?" He slows, but my legs wrap around him tighter.

"Yes! Please don't stop."

"Hmmm, my little innocent Bren welcomes the pain. Noted." He resumes his punishing strokes, and I hold on for the ride. Each thrust gets me intoxicatingly closer to my release. A few more deep strokes and I'm exploding around his cock in waves. This is my strongest orgasm yet. My legs tremble as he thrusts his way to his own release. His mouth dips down, and he latches onto my shoulder as he fucks me savagely. I feel the moment his dick throbs within me, my own aftershocks intertwining with his. When the sensation finally dissipates, we both lay there, unable to move— his dick still inside me.

Neither of us speaks a word. Several moments pass before he slides out of me, and the soreness is instant.

"Ah," I cry out again. Seems like my vocabulary has been fuckably reduced. I have no other words. Silas has fucked them out of me.

"Come on," he says as he gets out of bed and reaches for my hand.

I take it and let him assist me out the bed. I foolishly look back. Fresh red blood stains his expensive white sheets. My mouth drops, but no sound escapes. I look between my legs as if the blood could have come from anywhere else. Dried blood coats the inside of my thighs. Silas reaches for me again, but I'm mortified. I've heard of the whole popping the cherry thing, but I didn't expect to saturate his sheets like some sort of pussy sacrifice.

"Um ... sorry about your sheets. I can pay for them. I just got to go." I know if I'm covered in blood like the movie *Carrie*, then I'm sure his cock is wearing it. I need to get the hell out of here. I attempt to snatch my swimsuit from the floor, but strong arms grab me before I get the chance.

"Shut it. I'm not letting you run because of a little blood. What did you think would happen? Newsflash, I didn't exactly go easy on you." He chuckles. Only I can't find it in me to laugh with him.

"My little sex kitten wanted it rough. Stop freaking out. It's only sheets. So worth it." His banter fades when he sees the stupid tears begin to trickle down my face. The ones I didn't want him to see, but he wouldn't let me go.

"Stop, please." His voice softens, and that makes it worse. I'm ruining something that was seriously spectacular just moments ago.

He grabs my hand again and walks us to his shower. Without letting go of my hand, he turns on the water. When the temperature has heated to his satisfaction, he pulls me into the glass kingdom with him. His bathroom truly is a palace in its own right; only I'm too distracted by my own embarrassment to care.

"Look at me, beautiful," he says encouragingly. When I do, the gentleness in his eyes shakes my soul. He pulls me further into him and kisses me slowly. This kiss doesn't harness the wild passion like before. It's tender and sweet. He holds me close and continues to kiss me under the rain showerhead. I feel the moment some of the embarrassment begins to ebb away. Being held like this makes me desire things I can't have—like *him*.

Silas finally breaks the kiss, but only so he can wash me. I don't even mind that it's some woodsy manly body wash. It smells like him. He uses extra care when he uses the washcloth between my legs, but I still flinch. My swollen vagina is sensitive to the touch, and he notices. He pats softer and then removes the nozzle to aim the warm water just where needed. He holds it there, letting the warmness dull the ache.

"Too much too fast," he says almost to himself.

It's my turn to comfort. "It's fine, Silas."

He nods, but he doesn't look convinced. He steps further underneath the water to wash, and I watch as the water repels from his taut muscles. Worry creases his thick brows, and the mood change is apparent. My own embarrassment over the mess I made has taken a back seat to my concern about what he's thinking. I don't want him to have regrets. He turns away from me, leaving me to study his perfection freely. His back flexes and every etch of defined muscle is making me want him again—for him to erase whatever this heaviness is that is thick between us, suffocating any remaining bliss.

I massage his back similar to what he treated me to earlier. I ease my hand around his abs and play with the rock-hard ridges beneath my fingers. He truly has the body of a god. I bet women throw their panties at him, and I've just had a taste. He brings more than just looks to the table. He's the total package. His grip on my wrist halts my exploring, and I feel the tension before he even turns around.

"You have to stop before you make me hard again," he warns, turning around. He shuts off the water and reaches for a towel for each of us. He hands me one and begins to dry himself off. My insecurities resurrect tenfold. *Of course.* Why didn't I figure this out until now? That concern I read on his face was probably him wondering how he would go about kicking me out. The shower was just so I didn't leave his room wearing the evidence of my lost virginity. He doesn't want to get worked up because he's done. I foolishly thought he worried that he'd hurt me. Why the hell did he kiss me like that then?

I dry off in record time. No strings. Got it. It was fun, and now it's done.

"You have a regular t-shirt I can borrow? I'll return it; I just don't remember where I laid mine down at the moment."

I just need to get that shirt and get the hell out of here. I got what I came here for, so why does his dismissal feel like a slap.

"Of course. I'll grab you one in a sec."

He wraps the towel around himself and walks back toward the bedroom, so I wrap my towel around my body and follow. Instead of getting the shirt immediately, he begins to strip the linens from the bed. I listen as he makes a call to have them replaced. While he is on the phone, I head outside where we were to find my shirt.

"What are you doing?"

His voice startles me, but I continue my search. "Looking for my shirt so I can go," I answer, never looking in his direction.

"I told you I would grab you one. I just needed to get new bedding first. Why are you leaving?"

Is he for real?

"I'm not doing the whiplash thing with you, Silas. Tonight was great. Now I'm going back to my room," I huff. "Well, as soon as I get a shirt. Can you get that please?"

My tough exterior is slipping. Inside, my heart is crumbling into a million disappointed pieces. I got so carried away with the tender moments that I lost sight of what this actually was—a fuck.

"Great? That's what tonight was?" He takes calculating steps toward me, his face stern and questioning.

"Yes."

I don't know what else to say. He tilts his head to the side in disbelief, and I know that was the wrong answer.

"So what now? You give me your virginity, and now you're ready to run again?" Agitation radiates off him. "Why do you make me chase you? I said I wouldn't, and here I am yet again—chasing!"

"I didn't ask you to chase me," I spit. "You know what? Forget the shirt. I'll go back to my room in this damn towel."

"You didn't ask me to chase you? Says the woman running."

"Ugh," I grunt.

I spin on my heel. I'm done. I maybe get three

SILAS

steps away before I'm grabbed around my waist.

"Dammit, Silas. First, you go all cold and push me away in the shower, and now you want to keep me from leaving? If you're done with me, just let it be so. I gave you an out here. You didn't even have to kick me out."

"Is that what's been going through that imagination of yours? Creating fictional scenarios on how this would all play out?" He holds me tighter. "I was upset with myself, Brennan. I wanted to take it easier on you the first time. I pride myself on control."

"It's fine. I told you. It's what I wanted. The pain was ..."

"Was what?" he pushes.

"I don't know," I admit. "At that moment, it was pleasure too. Now I'm just sore."

"You have to learn your limits. I should have known better. My dick overruled my rational thought, and for that, I apologize."

"I don't want you to have regrets. I already feel bad about your sheets."

"Can you just forget about those stupid sheets? I don't regret my time with you, either, so get that misconception out of that pretty little head of yours."

"So now what? I'm not running."

"Now you bring your sexy ass back to my bed.

We'll ice your swollen pussy back to normal, so I can make a follow-up visit."

He winks at me, and just like that, the tension melts away. He picks me up and carries me to his now newly made bed. Only he doesn't toss me on it this time. He eases me down in the center before running his hand through the melted ice.

"Oh, that just won't do. Sit tight. I'll get more ice."

I don't want to ice my vagina, but if he thinks that will help, I'll try it. I didn't forget about the shirt, and I don't think he did either. Slick fucker just wants to keep me naked. He's asked me to stay, so I'll stay quiet about it for now. Just as he promised, he wraps some ice in a towel and holds it to my swollen pussy. The burn of the coldness is hard to tolerate until the numbness takes over. With a click of the remote, he turns off the light.

I don't know at what point I fell asleep, but I wake in the middle of the night with an arm around my waist. Snuggled against his naked form. Suddenly, this is all too intimate. This feels dangerously like the beginning of something one-sided. This may be a casual cuddle for him, much like the day in my cabin, but it's not for me. The reckless feelings stirring within me clue me in that I have to go. I remove his arm, careful not to wake him up, then grab my still damp swimsuit off the floor and put it on. At least if I run into anyone, it will look like I just came back from a twilight swim. I look back at the bed one last time as the moonlight shines across his still sleeping form. *Sorry, Silas.*

CHAPTER 14

Brennan

THE LINE TO GET OFF THE YACHT MOVES steadily as people disembark to explore the first port here in St. Maarten. The guests were given the earliest time slot to leave the ship, and now, based on rotation and seniority, the employees may exit. Because I work in the aft and it's closed for the duration we're in port, I get an off day. That one perk of working in Spankville couldn't have come at a more perfect time.

Last night was amazingly unforgettable. Even with the blood shedding, virginal sacrifice moment that humiliated the heck out of me, Silas was perfect. But just as he had foreshadowed last night, I ran. I could handle things between us being just about sex. Hell, I'm even a little curious about this spanking thing he's into, but I wasn't ready for his tenderness. The way he cuddled me and insisted I rest while he iced my vagina made me want things that are not in the cards for us. I never expected the rush of emotions that flooded me. It wasn't just sex for me. I could picture him being mine and us sharing a bed every night together. My frustration is with myself. I openly agreed that he would be just a fuck, and my stupid heart decided to change the rules.

Last night, my heart chose him, and I was incapable of having a say. It doesn't care that he's rich, powerful, and can have any woman in his bed. He's not mine to keep. The sad thing is, I can't admit my reasoning for jetting out of his room in the middle of the night. I can't describe how having his arms wrapped around me was symbolic of an hourglass—the time slowly running out until he'd let me go. I'd given up on the idea of happily ever after happening for me. No Prince Charming is coming to save me. I have accepted my fate ... the life destined for me. How dare he make me want more? How dare he make me want to find out what it feels like to be loved?

"Fancy meeting you out here," Seth says, startling me as I step off the ship. His mock sophisticated phrases are hilarious. I honestly need the laugh.

"Why are you just standing here on the docks? Were you waiting on me?" I tease.

"Actually, I was trying to decide what I wanted to do first since I hadn't originally planned to get off the ship." He shrugs. "What about you? Where are you headed off to?"

"No clue. Just thought I'd sightsee and take some pictures," I remark, holding up Silas's camera.

"That looks like a pretty expensive camera you got there, doll cakes. I'd better accompany you, so you don't get mugged."

"Ah, you want to protect me from all the potential thieves out there dying to get their hands on this baby?" I latch on the neck strap to secure it in my possession.

"Not you. The camera. Maybe I should carry it just to be safe."

"What about me? Am I not worth protecting? Are you saying the camera is worth more than I am?" My jaw drops in feigned shock.

"Okay, okay. I'll protect you too. Besides, who

will help with the work if something happens to you? I can't be responsible for your duties along with mine. Still, let me carry the camera just in case."

He flashes the brightest smile imaginable. I can't help but giggle. He is just what I need to pull myself out of this funk.

"You're such a weirdo, Seth. Here, I thought rich people were weird with all their kinky fetishes, but you're one odd duck."

He just winks at my conclusion of his wackiness. "Come with me to go window shopping. I might get the urge to splurge and may need you to talk me down."

"I'll go with you, but only to keep all the straight women off your scent. You're not helping with all that sex appeal you're flaunting."

Seth may be gay, but his masculinity is unquestionable. Muscles bulge from his jeans and fitted tee like a visual wet dream. Although he is painstakingly gorgeous and plays for the other team, my foolish blood-pumping organ has already been claimed. Still, I'm not visually impaired. The man is sexy.

"Okay, but if we run into any hot guys, I'm telling them that you're my baby sister."

"Deal."

We shake on it. He loops his arm through mine,

and we head to look at all the things we're not going to buy.

We spend the day together while I take random pics ... a lot of random pics. Like "someone should really take this camera from me" random pics. I didn't stick to just landmarks either. The dated buildings are so colorful and beautiful, each structure more visually stunning than the last. Seth blames me for not getting more window shopping done. I don't see the point, but it's fun for him. He says that he is getting ideas to recreate his wardrobe. I'm more focused on finding exciting things to capture with my lens. It's helping me keep my mind off Silas, and I'm getting more comfortable using the features. As I zoom in to capture a shot of a church in the near distance, I hear Seth's phone ring, and he curses under his breath. He answers, but the conversation is cryptic with only yes and no responses. He looks around before rattling off our location. He nods as if the person on the other end of the phone can see him. What the heck is going on? His call doesn't last long. He turns to me, and my hackles go up.

"I have to go. I've been summoned."

"Summoned? To do what and by whom?"

He looks genuinely disappointed, but I don't like

this nonchalant vibe he's giving me now. I want my over-the-top friend back who oddly likes to look at things he has no plans to buy.

"I wish I could tell you what, but I can't. A few of us were selected for a special assignment, and I'm bound by confidentiality. I have to go back to the boat. Please don't ask."

He gives me his saddest puppy dog eyes, and I melt. I can't say that I'm not more than a little bit curious, but I won't question him further. I respect that he's told me as much as he has.

"Fine. Let's go back."

"Actually"—a black Mercedes pulls up, interrupting his sentence—"that's your ride," he finishes.

"What? How? With who?"

"You forgot the last two w's—where and when," he adds, amused.

"Not funny! What in the ...?"

The driver of the Mercedes gets out and opens the back door. The heavily tinted windows make it impossible to see inside, but I reluctantly wave bye to Seth as he leaves in the opposite direction without answering my questions. Why couldn't he ride back with me? Where is he going? He's not headed in the direction of the ship. It would appear he has more secrets than he's telling me.

The driver just stands at the back door, waiting for me to get in. I hope I'm not being abducted because I have nobody to pay my ransom. Feeling assured that nobody in their right mind would abduct the poor, I walk over to get in the car. I'm not ready for the man I see waiting inside—Silas.

He lowers his designer shades down his nose to look at me, and my heart does a back flip. His tan jeans hug his muscled thighs while the rip at the knees shows a little bit of skin. His t-shirt showcases what I like to call chiseled perfection with every etch on display.

"Stop eye fucking me and get in, Brennan." His voice is firm, unwavering.

Suddenly, my escape from his bed last night plays on a loop in my mind, and I'm questioning just how pissed he is at the moment. He said he wouldn't chase me, yet he did, and then I ran. He can't be too pleased with me right now.

I ease into the seat next to him, unsure of what to say. The driver closes the door, and the vibrations carry with it the tension I feel. This is awkward. I didn't get this far in my thought process—like how I would feel when I saw him again. The air in the car is heavy, suffocating. I can feel him all around me, and he's not even touching me. As if reading my mind, his hand slides across the butterscotch leather to grasp mine. He pulls my hand back toward him, and my body instinctively follows until the heat of his hip presses against me.

"Relax, Brennan. I'm not mad. I felt the minute you removed my arm from your body. I let you go because that's what you needed. I gave you the space to digest everything we had done—which is also why I didn't push for more rounds. And because you were sore."

I melt into him, letting him be my comfort. Pathetic and as cliché as it may seem, I'm falling fast. There's no manual for this, and I have no clue what the hell I'm doing. I've never dated, let alone had feelings for anyone. Maybe it's lust or his skill at sex. Whatever it is, it's not something I predicted. His fingers intertwine tighter with mine.

"I don't know what to say, Silas."

"You don't have to say anything. I understand. If it means I get to have you underneath me again, we'll go slow."

"Okay." I don't miss his "again" statement. His intent is to fuck me again, and foolishly, I'm more than willing. We mutually agree to leave my disappearing act unexplored, but so many unsaid things lie between us. I don't want to think about the consequences of where this is *not* leading. I don't know how, but this devilishly handsome man has managed to find me on the streets of St. Maarten. I left my phone in my cabin, and he still found me through Seth. He says he doesn't chase, but he has it down to a science. Apparently just as much as I have with running.

"How did you know I was with Seth?" My inquiring mind won't give it a rest. "You're quite the detective."

"There's not much that gets by me, sweetheart, not to mention my paid eyes."

"So do you have paid eyes on me?" I ask jokingly, but then my intuition wipes the smile right off my face. Seth's admission about having a special assignment rocks me. *Am I it?* "Is Seth one of your paid eyes?" He stiffens next to me. His hesitation is barely noticeable, but it's there.

"No, he's not," he insists firmly. "My paid eyes are my security detail. What did he tell you?"

I need to tread lightly here. Seth didn't disclose anything, but am I even allowed to know he has a special assignment?

"Tell me? Is it something he was supposed to tell me besides that he had to head back? I didn't get anything other than that because your car showed up and he bolted."

"Nothing to tell. You both weren't supposed to leave the yacht. One team member is supposed to stay back in case the guests finish their touristy shit earlier and want to come back for a little bit of playtime." He brings my hand up to his lips and presses a soft kiss along my knuckles.

"I thought the aft was closed on days the ship was in port? I read that in the binder information."

As soon as the words leave mouth, I want to snatch them back and set them on fire with gasoline. He arches a single groomed eyebrow at me with a smirk that tells me he caught my slipup. That information was well within the "all the ways to make the ass red" binder he gave me. Now he knows just how much I've been reading—religiously, in fact—since that little nugget of info is somewhere in the middle of the binder.

He winks at me, and I just smile like someone caught with their hand in the proverbial cookie jar.

"Ah, been reading the book of knowledge, huh?" he guesses correctly. "Let me clarify. The aft doesn't close outside the normal ship hours of four a.m. That's just to allow time for things to be put back and sanitized for those who like morning play. The aft isn't closed; I just don't provide lessons on the day we port … It's a free day."

"So a free day for guests but not for employees?"

"Correct. Some employees, not all. Somebody has

to attend to the guests. It goes by rotation, so you need to get with Jacob."

We ride in silence, passing homes and not heading toward the marina where we disembarked.

"Where are we going?" First, he mysteriously shows up to pick me up, and now, he's whisking me off somewhere.

"The yacht doesn't leave until tomorrow morning. I like to rent properties for overnight stays when we're at a port for at least a day. I can take you back if you want. Should have asked if you'd mind joining me."

"I feel bad because I have no seniority, yet here I am. Whoever got stuck on board probably has a plethora of dirty words for me."

"Don't overthink it," he rebuts. He unravels his hand from mine and slides his fingers underneath my cotton white summer dress that skims just above my knees. I look in the rearview mirror to see if the driver is watching us. My heart fibrillates, and my breathing becomes labored.

"What are you doing, Silas?" I whisper-hiss.

"Bringing you peace."

His simple explanation revs up my libido, successfully distracting me from thinking about work. He has the word peace tatted on his right index finger … the finger that is inching its way closer to my pussy.

His inconspicuous promise invokes a tightening in my belly and opens the floodgates into my panties.

His "no-holds-barred, I do what I want" attitude is sexy as hell. I'm scared shitless to let him continue the path he's on, but a tiny thrill battles the fear with equal tenacity. Silas brings out my extrovert who likes to walk the line of kink. His fingers reach their intended destination, and I'm thankful I'm not wearing my grandma underwear.

"Still sore?"

"A little," I admit. "Every step reminds me of last night."

"Good!"

"Good?" I asked, knowing it's relevant for some macho achievement.

"Fucktastically good," he clarifies definitively. "I hate that I went all caveman on you for your first time, but it also means that you have to think about my cock every time you take a step. You can't run from that."

My tendency to run has made its way back into the conversation but not chastisingly so. He slides that wicked peace finger through my wetness as I lean back in the seat, spreading my legs to accommodate his ministrations. He has other ideas, though. He brings that same finger to his mouth and licks it slowly. My eyes follow enviously. I want to feel that talented tongue again.

"You're such a tease." I stick my tongue out at him. How dare he get me worked up and then leave me hanging?

"Patience, my little jelly bean."

"Jelly bean? Really? That's the nickname you're going with?"

"Why, yes. They're my favorite candy, and they remind me of you. Sweet and cute. Especially the freckled ones."

"Oh, my God, Silas. You're insufferable. Jelly beans are not cute, and they do not have freckles. I don't even have freckles, so I'm not sure where you're pulling that analogy from."

"Some of them do have freckles. Okay, speckled, but I like to think of them as freckles. I was saying they were the cutest out of the other jelly beans because they were different, just like you—special."

"I can't believe you're comparing me to candy," I joke. Funny how he can take me from horny to laughing. Influencing my emotions effortlessly.

"Not just any candy ... my favorite candy."

"Can I be the pink kind, at least?"

"Yes. You can be the strawberry cheesecake jelly bean with freckles."

He pulls me in for a kiss so much more passionate than what we shared last night. I pull him tighter as I crawl on his lap. I need to be in his arms. I might as well enjoy the ride before the inevitable crash.

CHAPTER 15

Silas

THIS IS THE MOST FUN I'VE HAD IN A WHILE. IT'S so easy to be around Brennan. No false pretenses, no expectations or ulterior motives. I get to just be a regular guy ... take a break from the multi-millionaire that has the weight of the world on his shoulders. For the first time, I'm questioning my own outlook on what I want personally. I've been down a similar road before, and it nearly broke me. My "love" key is my daily reminder to avoid such a pitfall ever again. Then Brennan appears, bringing a naïvety that is refreshingly pure and appealing. She gives me hope, insight to possibilities I once thought unattainable. I'm a different man when I'm with her ... a better man.

We ride with her cuddled in my arms for the remainder of the drive to the house. The car slows as it takes the secluded path that leads to where we'll be staying. Brennan bounces on my lap when the ocean comes into view.

"We're on the beach!" she giddily exclaims.

"Please tell me you've been to a beach before." She is so easy to impress. Simplicity at its finest. It makes me want to show her the world.

"Of course. Not often, but I've been before. Usually only for a couple of hours because that's all the time my mother could spare. We would ride the bus down to the beach, and once, we actually got to spend the whole day there. I would love to see the beach at night."

I rented a two-story home on the beach for the night. Now that she's joining me and has shared her excitement about the beach, I have a few other surprises up my sleeve. It's been a long time since I've wooed a woman—three years, in fact—but it's the first time I've wanted to. When the car finally stops, she is the first one out. She runs straight to the beach. I lag behind to make a few calls ... and set my plan in motion.

I'm happy to watch her kick off her sandals and let the sand sink between her toes. The sight tugs at my heart, but I wave it off. She runs back up to join me and jumps in my arms. I like carefree Brennan.

"Sorry. I may have gotten a little carried away," she surmises.

"Not at all. Come. Let's go explore the house." As if she has a choice. She's wrapped around me, and I'm not letting her down. I carry her into the house. We check out each room with her in my arms.

"This house is amazing." She smiles. "I love the airiness and all the natural light. Not to mention, you can see the ocean from every room."

"Well, what do you want to do first?" My guess is that she will want to go down to the beach. We have a little bit of time before my chefs come.

"Promise you won't give me crap if I tell you."

That gets my attention. "What?"

"Promise me, Silas. Promise me that you will just say yes or no."

"Okay. I promise. Now spill." She slides down off me and walks to look out the French doors.

"I want you to use your belt on me."

What the hell? I don't know what I was expecting, but it wasn't that.

"What? Why?" I admit my tone doesn't come

across as welcoming to the idea, and that's because I don't welcome that. Not like this. The belt is on the far end of the spectrum. Nobody starts there.

"You promised, Silas." She hasn't turned to face me.

"The answer is no then, sweetheart. If you've been reading what I left for you, then you know that the belt is at the end of the stingy spectrum. I can't start there not knowing your pain tolerance by using a shorter range toy with less sting first. That would be irresponsible of me."

"Okay. Let's go to the beach. It's such a pretty day."

She pushes open the French doors and begins the walk without me. *Fuck.* I have to damn near break into a jog to catch up to her. I don't stop until I'm in her direct path, blocking her so she has to stop.

"Hey. We're okay?"

"We're fine. Why wouldn't we be? I asked you to share a piece of yourself with me, and you said no. That's your right." She gives me a small smile, but it's forced.

Why did she have to phrase it like that? She asked me to share a piece of myself, and I said no after she shared such a big part of herself with me. I feel like the biggest dick right now.

"Come back to the house with me. I have

something else in mind." She doesn't answer either way, but she doesn't stop me from leading her back the way we came.

I walk her up the stairs to the master bedroom. She lets go of my hand and climbs on top of the poster bed. She looks at me expectedly, waiting for my next move. I pull my shirt off over my head, and her eyes narrow in, just as I expect them to.

"Take off the dress, Brennan." I purposely deliver the instruction as a demand.

She wants me to share this piece of myself, so this is her test. How she proceeds will determine which version of me she gets. I need to know that she can mentally handle what she's asking me for. She was just a virgin yesterday, for fuck's sake. Because she gave me her virginity, I will oblige her request only if she is able to give me her submission. There is no room for innocence or regrets—only conviction in her desires.

I watch as she gets down off the bed. Her eyes never leave mine as she slides the straps of her dress down her shoulders. She eases the dress the rest of the way off until she stands before me in a white half bra and cotton panties. I have to give it to her. Her pseudo confidence almost has me fooled, but the slight tremble of her body gives her away while she stands there in her virgin white undergarments. I have to give her credit for trying, though. She wants this. She wants me.

"Come here, baby." I finally break.

There's that ugly word again, but I don't give a shit. I can't even deny her. I can't give her the same test I've used to test the readiness of the other women I've played with. I take a seat in the chair near the window as she stands before me, waiting. I slide her underwear down her legs until her bald pussy is on display. I reach up and unsnap her bra with one flick of the front clasp between her gorgeous tits. They fall heavily. She is now naked, but she has yet to attempt to cover herself. She's giving me control.

I slide my fingers between her folds, back and forth, until her wetness coats my fingertips. "You want me, Brennan?"

"I want all of you. I want the parts you haven't shared with me."

"You have no idea what that part looks like, sweet-heart. You only think you do. You sure you want a taste?"

"I want all of you," she repeats.

"Well then, I will give you what you've asked for. Just know that I'm in charge. That's the only way this works."

"Okay."

And just like that, I remove the kid gloves. Too

bad I don't have access to my toys here, but I'll improvise. "Touch yourself, Brennan."

Her hands cup her breasts and squeeze softly as I continue to play with her pussy. My dick is already growing against my jeans. Time to see how much pain she can take. I'll only take her as far as her tolerance will allow. I'll have to be finely attuned to her body's cues since she doesn't know her limits.

I lean back in the chair and tell her to get across my lap. "I'm going to give you a sample of what I like."

She doesn't even hesitate to assume the position. She lies across my knees with that beautifully shaped ass finally within my grasp. I massage and caress, my dick getting more excited by the minute. The first strike is moderate, another test. She flinches, but then the most beautiful moan escapes from her. It spurs me on to increase my force, careful not to spank in the same spot.

"Mmmm … yessss!" she moans louder.

I allow my hand to slide down her pussy. She's soaking wet. I insert a finger in her still dripping heat to be sure. I'm right. She's not just wet; she had an orgasm. *Well, damn.* The angry red marks on her ass taunt me. I've left my mark. I've claimed her ass as mine, and now, I want to claim her ass. I rub her heated skin, need building within me to be her first in that way too. I don't realize I've pressed my finger against her tight hole until she answers my unasked question.

"Yes," she says simply.

"Yes? I didn't ask anything."

"You want to fuck me where your finger is, and I want all of you," she confesses.

She turns her head just enough for me to see the orgasmic smile she's wearing. Her lids are hooded. I help her up and back over to the bed. I slide my belt out of my jeans. She's given me so much and just came from me spanking her. I gave her a taste of my world, and she surprised me at how much she's enjoyed it this far. I have to know how she reacts to the belt. I won't push. We don't have to conquer all her firsts in one day, but I'm curious where she falls on the stingy scale.

I remove a condom from my pocket and place it on the bed—making my intent known. Afterward, I don't waste time removing my jeans. My dick springs free, ready to play. I bend her over the bed, no talking necessary. She sees the belt in my hand, and she's greedy for it. She stretches her arms across the bed and pushes her ass out.

"Your word is red, and I will stop. Understand?" She nods in the affirmative.

Good. She understands her safe word. I don't have plans to draw this out. Just give her a taste for being such a good girl. I want to give as good as I get. I deliver five blows in succession. She wiggles more than she did with my hand, but she pushes her ass out further with each strike. She meets the belt in anticipation. She wants more. I can tell. She fists the blanket and wiggles her ass in a plea for more, but that's enough for now. She already had ten swats from my hand before the belt. She will have two different distinctive red marks on her ass and soreness. I'll need to start the aftercare soon, so I need to fuck her now. My dick can't wait any longer.

"I'm going to claim your ass now, baby." She answers by pushing her ass out even further, bowing off the bed. She is still riding the high. *Perfect.*

I sheath my eager cock with the condom I placed on the bed. I place the tip of my dick into the entrance of her hot, wet pussy and use the wetness I find to coat her ass. I line myself up at her asshole as I spread her cheeks apart with my hands.

"Push out, sweetheart." I wait until she does before I slide into her tightness.

"Holy—" She grips the blankets tighter. I push further, inch by inch, allowing her to slowly accommodate to my size.

I lean over her body and palm her tits. I place soft kisses on her back. She pushes against me, gyrating her ass against my dick. My vixen has a kink for pain. This little discovery is optimal for us both. I can't believe my luck. For the first time since Jasper, I want more. I'm not sure what the "more" is, but I just know I want it with her.

She won't let me just hold her like this. She is topping from the bottom, demanding I get out of my head and get to fucking, so I oblige. I give her a few gentle strokes before I bury myself deep—deep enough for her dripping pussy to soak my balls. I let her set the pace because I don't want to hurt her. She is so damn tight. She bounces her ass on my dick in a tantalizing rhythm. I know I'm close.

"You feel so good, Silas. I'm about to come."

I can feel her legs shaking. I possessively want that nut on my dick. Without preamble or rational thought, I pull out of her ass, remove the condom, and dive into her heat. I reach around and massage her clit as my hips piston. I slam into her savagely, my own balls tingling—warning of my impending orgasm. She reaches that pinnacle first. *Thank fuck.* I let go of the nut I was holding back until she got hers. We come together beautifully in an orgasm of epic proportions. I let my cock throb, in no hurry to leave her magical depths. It's not until I slide out of her that I realize my mistake. *Shit.* I took the condom off. I can't even blame it on a concern for cross contamination. The truth is, I needed to feel her ... just her. I broke my number one fucking rule. I never fuck raw. I wasn't planning on fucking her as soon as we got here. With all the excitement of her enjoying a taste of my kink, I got a little carried away. The control I pride myself on has been challenged more than I want to think about right now. I know she's clean since I just took both of her firsts, but fuckedy fuck!

Panic begins to settle in my chest. What if I get her pregnant? What are the odds? I've always been so careful. Sensing my mood change, Brennan gets into bed and uses the come-hither motion for me to join her. I don't know if she realizes my slip up yet.

"Join me, baby," she urges as she gives my term of endearment back to me. I don't even bat an eye at the word coming from those lips. We only have about an hour of daylight left, so I know I need to finish prepping my plan. It'll serve as a distraction from my fuck up.

"Nah. I have a surprise I have to get ready for you. Just rest here until I get back. No leaving this spot until I come back for you."

"Oh, I love surprises," she informs me as she stretches out on the bed.

The sight of her lying on the bed in the obvious

afterglow and wearing my marks tugs on my chest. Little Miss Delavan has slipped past my wall, and now I need to decide what I want to do about it. I don't think I could withstand another outcome like the one I had with Jasper. Everything in me screams she is different, but this love key around my neck is screaming equally loud to proceed with caution.

"Get ready for a surprise to shame all surprises then, sweetness." She beams with excitement and her face flushes crimson. I watch as it trails down her body, but it's still not a match for the ones I created.

I wasn't planning this first surprise until much later, but now I can incorporate it with her aftercare. I throw on my jeans, foregoing the shirt to check the porch downstairs. My list of things has arrived. I look down the path leading to the beach and see my second surprise is underway as well. Let the wooing begin. My jelly bean is in for a special treat.

CHAPTER 16

Brennan

The smarting pain keeps me from lying on my back on the bed. I opt to lie on my stomach while I replay it all. I can't believe all that just happened. I don't even know what possessed me to ask to be spanked. I guess I've been harboring a curiosity from reading about all the kink in Silas's binder, but I was unsure if I would like it. I more than enjoyed it. What started off as pain dissipated into something euphoric and orgasmic. The question is,

SILAS

what does that say about me? What kind of freak gets off on pain? Apparently, I'm that freak. *Who knew?*

I didn't think he would give in to my request. He had a mini freak-out for going all caveman on me during my first experience with sex. He erects these protective walls around me that even shelters me from him. I don't want safe. I wanted a part of him, the essence of him, and he gave it to me in spades. I'd say he really gave it since I happen to know he forgot to wear a condom.

I'm afraid to bring it up. I don't want anything to ruin this bubble we're in. I'm pretty confident that he religiously practices safe sex. Stupid, but I trust that he is disease free. There is still the conception possibility, but those odds should be slim. I'm not on birth control, but I just had my period right before I came on board. Statistically, I should be safe. No need to freak him out.

The door creaks open, and I realize I didn't even know he'd closed it behind him.

"Take these, love," he tells me when he gets closer to the bed. He holds out a glass of orange juice and two circular white pills.

"What are these for?" I ask already taking the pills.

"They're arnica pills. They will help reduce the

bruising from our play. The arnica cream is for later and has witch hazel and menthol to help with the pain."

"Well, weren't you the presumptuous one. How did you know you would need all that stuff? Surely, you don't carry that around with you."

Silas

I see the moment that little light bulb she likes to turn on in her head clicks on. "Wait. It wasn't for me. You knew you'd be renting a place because you said you always do when you dock for at least a day. You were planning to bring someone else here to play with. *Boy, aren't I the lucky one.*"

I don't miss the sarcastic undertones. That mind of hers is just a little too creative sometimes. She invents these misguided stories and runs with them.

"Are you done with your foregone conclusion, Sherlock Holmes?" She tilts her head in disbelief. If her ass wasn't already red and sore, I'd spank her ass again for that off-base assumption.

"Enlighten me then."

"Babe, I have money. It's that simple. You'd be

amazed how quickly I can get things. Even when they're out of sight, I have people on my detail who cater to my every whim. I don't abuse it, but if I shoot off a quick text, stating I need some fucking arnica pills and cream, it gets done expeditiously."

"But when did you even have time?"

"You mean the time it took to send off a text when you asked me to share a part of myself with you and then bolted through the French doors? I sent the text because I knew you'd eventually get your way. You make me want to give you everything, Brennan."

I watch in satisfaction as that admission knocks the wind from her sails. She's not used to anyone treating her like the special woman who she is. She is so jaded and quick to think the worst because she doesn't believe she deserves better. It's her only flaw that needs work.

"I'm sorry, Silas. You've been incredibly sweet, and here I am assuming crap. I think my positivity compass is a little broken sometimes."

"Nah. Our perspectives are shaped by our experiences. Just know, I'm here to give you a new perspective."

Brennan

It's pointless. This man irrevocably, undeniably owns my ass—pun intended. Even after I question his motives, his sweetness for me doesn't waver. He says things that make me think just maybe he is falling for me too. He's letting some of his rules go for me. I'm in deeper than I was yesterday, and it frightens the hell out me. I can't get off this ride, though. I don't want to.

"Before the arnica cream, let's get you into your first surprise." He covers my eyes with his masculine hands and nudges me forward. I walk slowly since I can't see. I smell his surprise before I can actually see it. The smell of roses wafts in the air, much like the massage oil he used last night. He uncovers my eyes, and I swear, an inkling of fear melts away from my heart.

The vision before me is right out of a fairy tale. An inviting bath surrounded by varying sizes of candles awaits me. The water is opaque white with floating rose petals.

"It's a Cleopatra milk bath … fit for a queen. It's filled with goat milk, rose petals, rose oil, and vitamin E oil," he explains. "The warm soak will relax you and do wonders for your ass."

I could get used to this pampering thing. He's gone

above and beyond. Never in a million years would I have ever thought this would be my life. This gorgeous man doting on me, bending his rules for me.

"This is so sweet, Silas. Careful or I might begin to think you actually like me." Again, I've stuck my foot in my mouth. Why did I have to go and hint that this thing between us is more than a fuck? *Ugh.* "I mean think you actually like fucking me," I add. I try to clean it up, but it sounds worse.

Silas helps me into the bath. I lower myself slowly into the silky water and instantly feel relief.

"I love fucking you, Brennan," he finally answers. He gives me a warm smile, and I try not to read in his eyes what he's not saying. "Just relax and enjoy your soak. I'll be back for you shortly for your next surprise."

He returns within minutes with a red glass of wine. "Can't forget the wine."

I take the glass from him and take the first sip. It's somewhat tart but good. "Is this my other surprise?"

"No. I'm still working on it. I'll be back." And with that, he's gone.

I truly feel pampered. Something tells me this is not the normal Silas treatment. Is it because I gave him my virginity and now my first anal? I brush off the sense of obligation theory. I'm just going to enjoy all this and follow his lead. My heart is already invested, so it's pointless to come up with alternative explanations. I finish the glass of wine and set the glass next to one of the candles before leaning all the way back into the water. The only thing that could have made this soak better was for him to join me.

"Wake up, my little jelly bean." My eyes snap open, and I find a still shirtless Silas kneeling next to the tub. I have no idea how much time has passed. This soak really did relax me.

"Stand up, love. Let me wash you." I do as he asks. He rubs rose soap on a sponge and begins to bathe me. He's extra gentle when he washes my ass. "My marks look great on you. My dick is getting hard again just looking at them. The red is darkening now. I've claimed this ass in more ways than just one," he beams with pride.

"Yours," I answer in agreement, but he goes quiet. He finishes bathing me and even washes my hair before pulling a gigantic plush towel from the rack. I feel fully pampered.

I step out of the tub and let him wrap me up. As I'm drying my hair and body, he disappears and returns with a t-shirt.

"This all you get to wear today."

"Just your shirt, huh?"

"You don't need anything constricting against your ass. That and I get to watch you parade around in my shirt and know that you're naked underneath."

I want to kiss that smirk right off his face. He is just too cute for words. Especially when he is being all flirty and considerate.

He slides the shirt over my head and then kisses me on the forehead. "If it wasn't for this next surprise, I'd vote that you just be naked," he hints. Now I'm really curious about what he has up his sleeve. He takes his time rubbing the arnica cream on my ass—probably a little more time than necessary. I have no doubt he loves my ass.

"Have you seen my hair tie and bobby pins?" I ask, interrupting his medicinal fondling.

"They're somewhere in the trash." He shrugs his shoulder, unconcerned. "I'm boycotting them for the duration of our time here. Your hair is too gorgeous to be wearing a nun bun. Besides, you're no longer chaste, so I think it's false advertisement. No more of those chastity buns when you're with me."

That's it! Nun bun? Chastity bun? I've truly heard it all. I double over in laughter until Silas swats my ass. The sting gets my attention. "Let's get to your next prize, Princess Leia."

"Ha. She wore two buns, and I only wear one, so that kind of ruins your analogy there, stud."

"Well, since you'll be wearing zero buns, it's a wash anyway," he gloats. He gives me the sexiest smile, dimples daring me to disagree with him.

"Fine. I'll let this hair be wild and out of control just for you."

"Sounds like a marvelous idea. Glad you thought of it," he mocks.

His laugh is truly infectious. He'd better be glad he's handsome. I toss my damp hair over my shoulder for a flair of theatrics.

"Let's go, boss man." I can create pet names too.

The sun is setting behind the clouds. The orange and yellow hues fade into one in beautiful harmony. Silas leads me toward the beach; I'm guessing to watch the sunset. I did mention earlier that I wanted to see the beach at night. Only, I'm not prepared for fairy tale number two. This is the kind of thing that only happens in the movies.

A little table low to the ground with lanterns is surrounded by cushions and pillows to sit. A bottle of champagne is on ice with two flutes at the center of the table. More lanterns illuminate our little secluded spot on the beach in the shape of a heart. I can't help the tears that roll down my cheeks. I'm the luckiest woman right now. I take a seat on one of the cushions, and Silas cozies up next to me, wiping away my tears.

"Those are happy tears, I hope."

"Yes. I can't believe you did all this. You even created a heart for us."

I wish we could stay in this heart bubble forever, but I don't say that part. I'm desperately trying not to read anything serious into all this without him saying the words.

"The heart is just like your heart-shaped ass and face." He winks. He didn't say I had his heart, but it doesn't take away from how romantic this all is.

He pours us champagne, and I recognize the rose-colored bottle from our rendezvous last night. I swear he has an obsession for roses.

"What is your predilection with roses? Rose oil, rose soap, rose champagne … I'm sensing a theme here."

"Roses hold a variety of beneficial properties for the skin and can increase the libido. The flower itself can mean different things, depending on the color and how many you give to someone. Its symbolism appeals to me." He brushes a strand of hair from my face and tucks it behind my ear.

"So many people give roses without fully under-standing the statement they're making. I don't give any roses to people, but if I did, most wouldn't appreciate its significance," he adds.

Two men approaching in white chef coats and car-rying trays of food interrupt our discussion about ros-es. This night just keeps getting better and better. They organize the food on the table in front of us and fill our flutes with the champagne that's on ice. I still can't pro-nounce the name of it.

My stomach growls on cue when I take it all in. The presentation of the food makes it almost hard to eat it. It's so pretty, but I said *almost*. The chefs don't attempt any small talk. They place napkins in our laps and simply tell us to enjoy.

"So this is surprise number two. I have one more because I think things are better when they come in threes."

"Like orgasms?" I wink, stealing his signature move.

"Orgasm are better in multiples, not threes," he corrects, and I'm inclined to agree with him.

"Seriously, thank you for all this … for making me feel so special."

"You deserve nothing less, jelly bean." He leans over and plants a chaste kiss on my lips. "Now let's devour this food before it gets cold. Then we can move on to the finale."

We both have salmon and asparagus with cherry red tomatoes. I sip on my champagne between bites, telling him about all the pictures I took today. He tells me about some of the amazing places he's visited and how they would be great to get pics of. Is he offering to take me to those places? This is how life should be, simple yet memorable. We don't need fancy restaurants or extravagant outings for a perfect date. Can this be considered a date? Or is it just two people enjoying each other's company after some great sex and *impact play*?

I scrape my plate clean—no shame. I was hungrier than I thought. We really worked up an appetite with our bedroom activities. Without prompting, the chefs return to pour us more champagne and take away our empty plates. They offer dessert, but Silas waves them off because we're both stuffed. Were they hiding in the bushes, waiting until we finished? I have to give it to them. Their service is magnificent. Silas thanks them and wishes them a good night.

"Time for surprise three." I rub my hands together like a restless child.

Silas just laughs at my shenanigans. He pulls out an iPad from behind one of the pillows. Now I'm stumped. *What the mess?*

"So for the finale, Brennan, we're going to spend the night on the beach under the moonlight and stars. The waves will lull us to sleep until we wake to watch the beautiful sunrise." He raises that peace finger in the air. "First, though, I plan to give you those multiple orgasms that I was just talking about. And once we're both spent, we will choose a movie to watch on the iPad with you cuddled in my arms. Tonight, there will be no running."

And my stupid tears are back. "That all sounds perfect. The perfect ending to the perfect night. Are these movies on Netflix by chance?"

"Yes. Some of them are. I'll even let you pick." He adjusts our pillows and cushions, so they merge as one. "Why do you ask if they're on Netflix?"

"Because this can now be considered the 'Netflix and Chill' part of the date." I'm rewarded with more of his gorgeous laughter.

"Oh sweetheart, there is only one flaw to that plan."

"What is that?"

"It's the Chill and the Netflix part of the date. I'm not waiting another minute to fuck you."

He leans me back and begins to remove his pants to prove his point. I hope those chefs really are gone. I smile because he agreed this was a date.

"Okay, but I choose *The Notebook*," I warn.

"Baby, just let me inside that pussy of yours, and I'll watch whatever sappy shit you choose. Tonight is your night. Let me show you just how much."

The minute he is naked and on top of me, I can't think about anything else. I don't know what will happen tomorrow, but tonight, he's all mine, and I'm his. No matter the outcome, this will be the most memorable night of my life. Well, second to losing my virginity to the sex god with hidden romantic tendencies. Tonight, I'm his exception.

CHAPTER 17

Silas

YESTERDAY WAS INCREDIBLE; UNCHARTED territory, for sure. I'm not too blind to notice something changed between me and Brennan. The thing is, I can't ignore it either. She had a few of her own slipups that indicated she was ready for more. Am I even capable of more? We ride back to the ship in silence, not touching—an apparent contrast to how we arrived at the house yesterday. It's like we're leaving our fantasy behind.

"Are you hungry?" I ask, desperate to penetrate the silence.

"I'm good. We just had that feast of a breakfast a few hours ago," she points out. More silence.

"Do you think it's wise for us to pull up together? What if people see us? What will they think?"

"Well, if they think I fucked you, their assumption will be right," I taunt. The truth is, I don't give two shits what they think. I write the checks. She has no reason to worry either, but I can understand why she would be.

"I'm serious, Silas. First, the newbie gets to get off the ship, and then I return with you. They're going to hate me."

Her fingers knot together in that nervous thing she does, and it pisses me off. She is still worried about how others see her rather than owning what she wants. I have to be considerate here, and it's testing my restraint.

"Okay, jelly bean. What do you propose?" I know what she is going to suggest before the insanity leaves her mouth.

"Let me out a mile before we get back to the boat, so I can walk on with everyone else."

"Fuck! You're not walking a mile to the yacht, Brennan. I'll give you a block, and I won't budge on this. Say no, and we'll pull up to the marina together," I huff.

"Fine. A block then."

There is no more talking. I'm afraid of what I might say. I opened my heart up to her—maybe not completely yet, but more than I have to anyone since Jasper—and it feels like a damn kick to the gut to watch her choose what others will think rather than just be with me. I'm not trying to hide my involvement with her, but she's hiding me. That's a fucking first, and it doesn't feel great.

I let her out as promised before we arrive back at the yacht. I don't do much more than wave her off.

The driver opens the door for her, but I remain inside, unseen. When we drive off, reality begins to creep back in. Our moment gone. This is the sign I needed. I grasp the key around my neck—my reminder. Time to get back to status quo. I have my rules for a reason. I'd do well to remember that.

I'm back on the boat and in my suite in no time. It's nearly noon, so the guests will begin to arrive back soon for our three p.m. departure. I head straight to my shower. I'll let the hot water wash away my disappointment. The rain showerhead pelts down on me as I close my eyes. I'm determined to let all thoughts of her go. That is until small feminine hands touch my chest.

My eyes fly open, and my first thought is that Tory has invaded my space. I'm just about to yell at her until I look down and see Brennan. She doesn't have a key card to my room, but my deck is still open to the pool below. She is naked and in the shower with me. There are so many unsaid words between us, but neither of us speaks. Our silence from the car continues.

Brennan drops to her knees, the water raining down on us both. Her mouth is so close to my cock now, her breath enough to make it harden in anticipation. She wraps a hand around my growing length and delivers the most tantalizing licks, balls to tip. My hands fist her hair as I resist the urge to fuck her mouth. She continues her unhurried pace, slowly wrapping that hot wet mouth around the head of my dick. She sucks and pulls with just the right amount of suction. Watching her give me head is sexy as fuck.

"That's right. Suck my dick, baby. Show me what you came to my suite for." My encouragement motivates her. Rewards her. She takes me just a bit deeper. Her hands stroke the length she still can't reach.

"Hmmm," she moans around my cock. I feel the vibration down to balls, and my control snaps. I begin to move until our rhythm is in sync. My toes curl against the travertine floor as I fuck her mouth. She jacks and sucks until I feel the buildup down deep in my balls.

"I want to explode in your fucking mouth, Brennan. If you don't want my load down your throat, you'd better take me out of your mouth now."

I give fair warning, but she shakes her head in protest. Instead, she sucks with even more determination. She massages my balls with one hand while continuing to suck me savagely and jack me with the other hand. She is greedy for my nut, and boy, do I deliver. I come so hard that I have to brace myself against the shower wall with one hand. And holy fuck me. She doesn't stop. She takes all my cum like a pro, continuing to suck as my dick throbs in her mouth. My legs tremble slightly while she drains me dry. She licks the last drop off her lips, and I'm impressed. If that was her apology, it was a fucking brilliant one—one that I can't refuse.

She rises slowly, and I help her to stand. She gives me a small smile, unsure. My brazen jelly bean.

"That was the best surprise ever, baby. That little mouth of yours is magnificently talented. You get all gold stars for that blowjob."

"Yes, teacher." She giggles.

I have to chuckle too when I get the gold star and teacher reference even though that wasn't my intent. I'm just glad to hear her giggle again. I don't like when we have tension between us. Just when I think I know what I need to do or how things should proceed with her, she renders me unsure. I'm not used to having to make decisions involving emotions. The answer is always so simple—don't!

"I'll just have to see what other lessons we can think of," I suggest.

"Sounds like a plan to me. I have to shower for real now. I have to work soon. I'm meeting Seth for a smoothie before our shift starts."

I step aside. "Shower away, but I get to watch."

She grabs the soap, and just as I warned, I watch her like the creeper she brings out in me. Those red marks on her ass call to me, begging me to inflict more. My hands wander over to caress her ass on their own accord. I can't tame the territorial feelings building within me. An overwhelming need to claim her ass again is too great. I grab some of the rose oil I keep in the shower and massage her asshole, giving an ample hint at what I want. She pushes her ass out toward me as an invitation.

That's all the encouragement I need. I remove the soap from her hands and place them to brace the wall in front of her. Without preamble, I bend her over, massage some oil on my cock, and then slide into her ass. She is still so tight. I reach around to massage her tits with one hand and rub her clit with the other. She continues to brace the shower wall with one hand, but claws at my thigh with the other. Her head falls back against my shoulder as little moans from her echo in the shower. She pushes against with every stroke, desperate to take every inch I give. I slide a couple of fingers inside her now swollen hot pussy. I finger fuck her as I drive passionately into her ass. She won't last long. I thrust into her harder, each stroke driving deeper than the last.

"This is mine," I growl as I pump. "You are mine."

Fuck it. I can't fight the inevitable. I want her, and I won't let anyone else have a chance. She is mine.

"Yours," she echoes for the second time since we left the beach.

My balls hitting against her pussy sound over the noise of the shower. Our race toward an orgasm has a rhythm. I insert another finger inside her so that she is completely full. I flick her G-spot, and like a tsunami, she squirts all over my fucking hand. Her juices are enough to pull me over the edge with her. I bury my nut deep inside her ass as I give it a few slaps. This earns me another squirt from her. We both ride out our orgasm under the showerhead until we are spent.

Just as I slide out of her, I get a clever idea. "Bend over further, sweetheart."

She does as I instruct, but her eyebrows knit in

confusion when I step out the shower. "Stay just like that," I reiterate.

I rush to my room and rummage through my bag of toys until I find what I'm looking for. I bring the package back with me so she can see that it's unused.

"It's a butt plug, sweetheart. And no, I didn't get it for anyone in particular before you ask. I'm a bit of a freak, and I have a collection of toys."

"Okay. But what are you going to do with it? I can't miss work, babe. I won't slack on my responsibilities because I'm fucking the boss," she insists.

She is still bending forward, and I'd be lying if I said I wasn't enjoying watching her submission to me. Even though I'm awakening her kinky nature, she still has quite a bit of naïvety left in her.

"Hmmm. Glad to hear you feel that way, but this plug is for you to wear to work."

"Huh?"

I take the small butt plug out of the package and get back into the shower with her. I ease the toy into her ass and then ask her to stand straight once it's secure.

"How does that feel?" I grin.

"Full." She blushes. "It feels like I have a dick in there. Is that why you wanted me to stay bent over? So you could put your butt plug thing in me?"

"In part, love. I'm much kinkier than you give me credit for, though. Remember you said you wanted all me?"

"Yes."

"Well, I'm just getting started. You see, the purpose of you remaining bent over is so that my cum didn't leak from your ass." Her eyebrows disappear into her hairline when she realizes my plan. "The butt plug will ensure that it remains there. You'll be taking a part of me with you to work, knowing who has claimed you—who owns you. With every step, the fullness will remind you of my cock!"

"So nobody will know? Just me?"

"Just you!"

She pulls me under the running water and kisses me passionately. I like that she has these little brave moments when she takes what she wants unapologetically. We need more moments like these.

"I can't be late, but I get off at eleven p.m. Can I see you then?"

"You'd better. You don't get to remove that butt plug until it's being replaced by my dick." I wink before kissing her on the forehead.

I turn the water off, and we both step out. She dries off quickly then puts on her uniform. She must have stopped by her cabin first to grab it. She came here strictly to get me off before her shift, and I admire her taking the initiative. It shows she was just as unsettled with our ride back to the yacht as I was.

I'm content to just watch as she puts her hair into that nun bun, as I call it—erasing the evidence of my undercover freak. *My freak.* That bun shit has to go when she comes back later tonight. I smile to myself just thinking about her dual personality—the kinky one that I have awakened. Once she's ready, she kisses me one more time before heading the way she came in. I'll have to talk with Atticus today. I need Tory's key card access voided and to get one for Brennan. Unlike the half-ass sneaking I did with Tory, I won't hide Brennan.

We've acknowledged her being mine and me being hers, but tonight, we need to discuss exactly what that means. No assumptions or misconceptions. What do we both want? I'm finally ready to take that next step with someone and potentially remove this key from around my neck. This is monumental. Now to get to work to make tonight just as special and to find a way to get her to agree to get off work a little earlier.

CHAPTER 18

Silas

MIGHT AS WELL GET THIS OVER WITH. I SEND out a quick text to Atticus to have him meet me at Hedonistic Lair in thirty minutes, instructing him to bring Brennan with him. I send the same message to Tory, but her request is to meet me in fifteen. I know the last time she came to my room, I told her it was over. Foolishly, I never asked for her key card to my suite back. That may have left things in a contradictory state, so I need to make a clean break, and more importantly, I need be more transparent with her about my growing feelings for Brennan. Although we were never more than fuck buddies, I owe her that much. Our time meant something, just not what she wanted it to. She will have to come to terms with our strictly professional relationship and accept Brennan's place in my life. If not, I will have no choice but to have her part ways with *The Playboy's Lair* or any of my other entities.

I dress in jeans and a black t-shirt. Something ominous lingers within me, but I can't quite put my finger on it. It's just a vibe I'm getting. I don't question my decision concerning Tory, but am I moving too fast with Brennan? I shake it off and head to the club. When I arrive, Tory is already waiting.

Eager.

Hopeful.

Shit.

Excitement to see me dances in her eyes as she gives me the widest smile. She tosses her hair over the shoulder of her black spandex dress. Her Louboutin heels clack against the marble floor, drawing my focus to her long legs. She is pulling out all the stops. I bought those heels for her a while back because I wanted those red bottoms wrapped around my neck while I fucked her. I wanted her ass to match that shade of red. She indulged in both stingy and thuddy play with me that night. She wants to mentally take me back to that time without saying a word. *Well played, Tory. Well played.* Too bad my mind is not that weak. It'll take more than a little trip down memory lane to derail this talk.

"Tory, I need my room key card back," I say before she can get any closer. I watch as the color drains from her face.

"So you're really doing this, huh? Is it her?" Her voice is deceivably calm. That's always her first question—*Is it her?* Today I will finally lay that accusation to rest.

"I won't bullshit you, Tory. I said we needed to end things before, but yes, I have growing feelings for Brennan."

"Feelings as in relationship feelings? The kind that you insisted weren't part of the deal with us—the kind you said you weren't capable of?" Her poker face is beginning to crack.

"Don't make this more difficult than it has to be," I warn. "Like I said before, we've had some incredible times together, but now we have to be over. Respect that and move on."

"So I was never good enough? These designer clothes you kept me in, the sadistic shit I encouraged, none of it was enough? I would have done anything for you … for a chance to have what you're giving her after only knowing her just two weeks."

Tears run down her face, and for once, the always-put-together Tory doesn't try to stop them. Black mascara stains her cheeks. I'm not a fan of hurting women, so the guilt gnaws at me. What could I have done differently? I was always honest with her.

"Tell me this, Silas," she continues. "If she is the type of woman you're into, homely looking, then why bother making me over to this?" She points at herself. "I was already her. I was the plain Jane maid. You made me into who I thought you desired, and now you're throwing me away for the same thing you created me from."

"Tory, I …"

The clacking of more heels and clapping interrupts my frustrated response. It takes a minute for my eyes to adjust. I do a double take because surely my eyes are fucking with me right now. *Holy fucking hell!* Even with bleach blond hair to mask her natural red, I'd know those green eyes and body anywhere. It's fucking Jasper. As she twists her ass in my direction in Louboutin stilettos similar to Tory's, my mouth goes dry. Crazy how I've never realized just how much her figure resembles Brennan's, only she has a little less ass. She is a damn bombshell, and the only woman to ever break me. How in the fuck did she get on my yacht?

"No hello for me, Silas?" She just turned my world upside down with her unexplained appearance, and she wants to coyly ask me about a hello?

I pull out my phone to get security just as Kassius comes running through the door. "Jasper is ..." The words die on his lips when he sees her. "Here," he finishes.

"I can see that. The question I want answered is how the fuck is this possible," I yell. I run my hands through my hair. My jaw clenches, my control hanging on by a thread.

"I'm right here, Silas," Jasper points out. "Why not just ask me how I managed to get onto your secret ship without you knowing?"

Tory looks on in confusion. I never told her about Jasper. She was part of my past before I built this business. I don't entertain her sarcasm. I'm on the phone trying to piece together how in the hell this happened.

"Who are you?" Tory finally asks, sensing the shitstorm that has just erupted.

Before she can answer, Atticus enters, and fuck my life, he's brought Brennan with him like I asked. She looks around the room, unsure of what she just walked into. Fucking hell, I forgot to cancel him bringing her. Jasper continues, ensuring my demise with Brennan before we even begin.

"I'm Jasper, Silas's first love; well, according to him," she announces. "And from the conversation I walked in on, I'm guessing you were supposed to be some sort of substitution for me. You see, I was the help. Still am, actually, and partly how I got the invite on this cruise. Look at me."

She spins in a circle. The fitted spaghetti strap dress shows off all curves. And oh, are they plentiful, more so than I remember. "I'm a maid for a very rich woman. Imagine my luck when said woman could not accept her invite because she just got engaged. She couldn't possibly let the new fiancé learn about the kink she was into, so she agreed to let me take her place."

"I'm nobody's substitution," Tory huffs.

"Afraid so, sweetheart," she challenges. "I over-heard you say he had taken up with another maid—a plain Jane, I think you called her."

"Housekeeper," Tory corrects. No snappy come-backs. She wipes the tears from her mascara-stained face.

"Tomayto, tomahto, dear. My point is, Silas loves a good rags-to-riches story where he gets to play the spoiler. He acts as if money isn't important, yet he splurges to impress you—to get you to succumb to him. He recruits you to be his makeover project without you knowing. He plays with you until he's bored or the next project catches his eye. What's her name? Brennan?"

"Enough," I boom.

This hypocrisy has gone on long enough. I let her talk while I investigate who dropped the ball, but she has crossed the line. None of what the fuck she's saying is true. Is that what she actually thinks?

"Everyone get the fuck out except Jasper and Atticus."

I need to get her off this yacht. We're almost two hours from our last port. We can't turn around, and we prefer to have my helicopter land when we're stationary.

"Fuck you, Silas," Tory yells with renewed tears. "Hope your game with me was all you wanted it to be."

"I want off this stupid fucking boat." I hear Brennan's sobs across the room. "Let me go, Seth. I mean it," she cries as she tries to tear herself away from his grip.

"Who in the hell is Seth?" Tory and Jasper ask in unison. That gets Brennan's attention. She stops struggling against him, and her eyes crinkle in confusion.

"That's Silas's cousin Kassius," Jasper informs, amused as to the reason for the misidentification.

This shitstorm just got exponentially worst. I initially asked him to help keep an eye on Brennan because she was the only new person. I needed to be sure she wasn't sent to infiltrate my lair to gain intel. I trust Atticus, but I don't know his friend who asked that she suddenly be transferred with little notice. I knew once I actually spent time with her I had nothing to be suspicious of. Only I never expected Kassius to befriend her. I would have confessed the truth before asking her to be with me, and now, I'm sure that will never happen. Tears of devastation roll down her flushed cheeks. I've caused enough tears today, and it fucking guts me.

"So your real name is Kassius?" Brennan's voice trembles. He nods in the affirmative. "Are you even gay?"

"No," Kassius confesses. "But our friendship was real. Everything—"

"How could you even say that?" She cuts him off. "Everything you told me about your background was a lie. I let my guard down and told you things when you fed me lies in return. What was the point? I asked Silas if you were one of his paid eyes. I guess since he wasn't paying you, it was okay to omit the truth. I believe this Jasper woman when she says I was another one of your projects—a game!"

She sniffles and begins to unbutton her collared

work shirt. What the actual fuck? Atticus tries to stop her, but she pushes his hands away. The room looks on, stunned silent. She doesn't stop until she has the shirt off—wearing only her bra and pants.

"I quit. At the next port, I want off this fucking ship. Game over."

She storms off, and I know better than to chase her right now. Kassius and I both betrayed her, and I have to make this right, but first, I have to get this situation under control.

"Karma is a wicked bitch," Tory says as she storms out.

Jasper just claps again, obviously proud of the havoc she's caused.

"Why are you here? I'll give you two seconds to explain yourself before I kick your conniving ass off my yacht!" I see red and not the kind I get off on. Livid is child's play at this moment.

I see Atticus and Kassius backing away to give us privacy. "Get to the bottom of this now!" I growl. "Somebody will be losing their job over this. I want answers by the time I finish here."

The two men nod, but they don't dally. My rage can barely be contained right now. I turn my sights back on Jasper.

"Answer my goddamn question," I fume. I'm on

her within seconds.

"Fuck you and your macho bullshit dominance," she challenges. "I snuck onto this stupid kink ship because I'm still in love with you. I've tried to move on, but you're in every man I see. Even though you played me like you did with those other two women, I foolishly can't let go."

"Are you mad? Or just plain delusional? You fucked us up. I was ready to give my inheritance up for you—all because you thought money defined me. I was willing to give it all up to prove I just wanted you," I huff. "You told everyone on my campus that day that you just wanted to fuck a college guy because high school guys were lame. You told me I was a pretentious prick and that you were bored with me. I tried for months to get you back—trying to prove how little money mattered. You fucking broke me."

She was eighteen and in high school, and I was a twenty-one-year-old junior in college. People thought I was a damn pedophile even though she was of legal age.

"Are you really going to play the victim here? I know the truth, Silas. Thanks to your stepsister back then."

"What are fucking talking about? What truth? Enlighten me please," I bite out.

For the first time since this whole debacle, her bitchiness fades. Her shoulder drop in defeat, and her eyes grow weary. She turns away from me, but I can hear the sobbing through her words, the wrack of her chest as they rip through her. *Fuck.* I can't deal with all this fucking crying.

"My mother taught at the private school, yet we didn't have the money you rich kids had. We barely made ends meet. When your stepsister, Jessica, became my friend, I was suddenly the cool kid. I was in with the popular crowd. Only the joke was on me," she weeps. "She thought my mother would give her good grades if we were best friends. When that didn't happen, she enjoyed telling everyone that she got her college brother to pretend to like me to sweeten the deal—that you actually had a girlfriend, and I was your high school pity fuck. I was the butt of everyone's joke. I dropped out of school, Silas. That scene on your campus was my last-ditch effort at revenge."

I'm shocked speechless. Flabbergasted. All this time, we've been apart due to a fucking misunderstanding. Jessica was a demonic bitch just like her mother. My father divorced her mother shortly after all that, so I never heard about this until now. Jasper's sobs are uncontrollably loud now. I want to hold on to the anger that I'm feeling. I want to hate her for setting all this in motion, but this is all starting to make sense. My stepsister's evil scheme not only derailed someone's life, but it also ruined what could have possible been for Jasper and me. I can't ignore what she must have gone through, especially after dropping out of school.

Reluctantly, but knowing it's necessary, I go to her and wrap my arms around her from behind. This is all so fucking unfortunate.

"None of that was true, Jasper. I was madly in love with you. I haven't been able to have a real relationship since. I tried three years ago, but I doubted her at every turn. I questioned her interest in my money until she finally had enough. This fucking key around my neck that I wear is because of you."

I spin her around so she can see the word love written on the key. "It's a daily reminder to myself to never give anyone my heart again because then I give them the power to break me. You did that to me. You broke my ability to love freely."

I leave out the part that I was entertaining removing the key for Brennan. Not because I'm in love with her, but because I wanted a real chance to discover that possibility. I don't like how Jasper infiltrated my space, but I get why. We've both been living with hurt and lies that have kept us from moving on with other people. That ominous feeling that I got before meeting with

Tory has come to light. Now I'm unsure again. Jasper's presence makes me question everything. I have to be sure. I don't know what I feel right now, and that's not fair to Brennan. The only thing I am sure of is that I can't leave things the way they are. She gave me the most beautiful gift, and in turn, I betrayed her with my omissions.

"I'm sorry, Silas. I should have just talked it out with you. It could have saved us both years of heartache. It's just, at the time, I was too broken. I still am. It was so believable because why would a rich, gorgeous college guy have any interest in a poor average high school girl unless it was a game like Jessica said. When you bought me things to wear, I thought it was so you wouldn't be embarrassed by me. I had been spiraling ever since. I work for a good woman now, close to my age, in fact, but I knew I had to find a way to see you again. Even before I knew the truth, I just couldn't go another day without trying."

"You were never average to me, and the money never mattered. When I bought you things, it was because I was trying to be a doting boyfriend. It was how I knew to show you I was falling in love with you."

I squeeze her tighter. It saddens me that she was willing to seek me out even when she thought I could be that cruel. It speaks volumes about her self-esteem

and what she thinks she deserves. She could also be totally playing me right now. Back to fuck me over for a
second time. She said she was a maid now. What if she
decided to look me up because now she wants access
to my money.

I don't want to assume shit because that's why
we're here now, but I can't be gullible for love again. So
do I even still love her? I'm afraid to answer that question. I need to dig deeper and get answers ASAP. I'm at
a fork in the road, and for the first time, I don't know
which path I want to take.

CHAPTER 19

Silas

"So are you going to kick me off your yacht now?" I can feel her respirations falter. She's holding her breath, at my mercy for an answer.

I let go my embrace. I just felt that I needed to hug her when she broke down in front of me. A moment of weakness urged me to comfort her. Her recall of that day took me to a place of vulnerability. I need to be objective here. I can't show my hand … the one that exposes just how unsure I am.

"I won't sugarcoat things. I'm more than a little upset by your approach and by the fact you were able to come aboard so easily. I pay handsomely to have my privacy and my safety protected. Not only did you sneak aboard, but you maliciously unraveled relationships I've created. You've hurt two people who didn't deserve that ambush by your version of the truth."

"What are you saying, Silas? Do you hate me?"

"Goddamn, I'm saying your intrusion into my space was enough. You could have come to me and told me all the things you were holding in. Yes, I would have still been pissed, but now, how can I trust your intentions? What do you really want from me?"

"I fucked up. I was desperate. I am desperate." She wipes away her renewed tears, finding a seat to sit on before pouring out her story.

"I never stopped following your life, Silas. I kept tabs on your success and your many appearances in those ritzy magazines. Deep down, I think I realized that maybe I was lied to, but I had to know for sure." She draws imaginary circles on her thigh with her French tip nails; anything to avoid looking at me.

"I'm a maid for a young socialite by the name of Ellie Daniels. She was the one who received your coveted invite. We have a good rapport, and she doesn't treat me like the help. She explained that she had been on your waitlist since you started these cruises. Only she couldn't accept because she had since gotten engaged and hadn't shared that part of herself with her fiancé. She knew she would be pushed to the bottom of your list if she declined, so she was more than willing to let me go in her place. I suggested it after I had realized it was *your* cruise. I accepted on her behalf, used my street hook up to get fake identification with her name, and dyed my hair to look like her as much as I could."

"What the hell? Why would this Jessica person go along with that fucked-up plan? I will ban her ass from all my entities and put her on a watch list with my connections as well," I fume. I'm beyond pissed off now at the amount of deceit that went into this treachery.

"She has no idea, Silas. I told her that I would respond and ask if the invite could be transferred to me. Only I lied to her—my friend. I saw that invite as a sign; my last chance to see you again. I did what I thought was necessary to ensure that I got on this boat. If I was wrong about that day, you needed to hear from me how sorry I was and how much I still loved you. Haven't you ever been tempted to do something bat-shit crazy for love?"

"I need some time to think about all this. I ask

that you go back to your cabin and not interact with my guests. I will send for you when I'm ready to talk again."

I can't even look at her right now. If what she says is true, I reserve an inkling of understanding for her desperation. That doesn't mean I can overlook what she's done, though. I listen attentively as she gets up and the sound of her heels move toward the door before pausing.

"I depleted my entire savings to be here, Silas. To dress the part of the role I was playing. You see, it was never about the money for me either. None of it means anything when you have a persistent void and are suffocating in sorrow because the one person you love is potentially moving on with someone else. That was the reason for hurting those two women. They've had parts of you that I've been suffering for years without. I love you with everything that I am. If you choose to kick me off your boat, I will go knowing that I did everything I could. If you tell Jessica what I did, I will lose a friend and my job. Again, there was no other recourse for me. I played all my cards—all in, for a chance to tell you how I feel."

The door opens and closes. I'm stunned speechless once more. My heart rattles around my chest with a familiar tug that I don't want to welcome. I don't want to still love her. What the fuck am I going to do?

Brennan

Rage still heats my flesh. The fact that I removed my shirt in front of those people is of no consequence. Every single one of them is a stranger—people I hope to never see again—so it doesn't matter. Was my exit dramatic? You bet your ass it was. I couldn't bear to wear his company shirt a minute longer. Had I been wearing the company pants instead of my own black slacks, they would have seen my bruised ass too. Lucky for them, I didn't launder my work pants before I left the boat. Oh and that fucking butt plug was taken out as soon as I made it back to the room. As his cum oozed from my ass, it was like a cleanse. My body ridding itself of the remains of him. He will soon be just a memory.

I feel like such an idiot. I was played and lied to by two people who had come to mean the world to me. I'm truly alone now. The anniversary of my mother's death was a little more tolerable because I had Silas as a distraction almost from day one. I hate him. I hate Set ... Kassius ... whatever the hell his name is. Are people's feelings really that insignificant when you're rich? I don't even know where I'm going to go or how long the money I have saved will last.

Alone in my cabin, I can finally allow the breakdown that has been on the brink from the moment I overheard Tory and then that Jasper woman. Looking at the two of them, how did I ever stand a chance? I can't stop the tears that bring me to my knees.

A knock on my door cuts through my gut-wrenching sobs. I don't want to talk to anyone on that side of the door. They can all fuck off as far as I'm concerned. I'm holding out judgment for Atticus until I know his role in this twisted game of deception. The knocking gets more persistent, but I don't budge from my spot on the floor. The telltale beep of a scanned key card has me kneeling with my head on the floor in defeat. I know it's him without even looking up, and I don't want to see him.

"Goddamnit," he curses. "Brennan, get up!" I don't move. I don't speak. I want him gone. "Please, Brennan," he tries again.

Still, I remain a mute statue. I sense him hovering over me, getting closer. I scurry closer to the night table near the bed. "Don't you fucking touch me," I snap. "You fucking maid collector."

I already quit, so I don't give a shit what I say. He

deserves worse.

"Stop. Surely, you don't believe the things Jasper said. Yes, I put eyes on you when you first got here. Seems my trust issues are warranted after the shit she pulled to get on this boat, but I never meant to hurt you. Everything between us was real. You made me feel, Brennan. Feelings that have been dormant since Jasper. You made me want to relax my rules with you."

"Well, now she's back, so you can just go live happily ever after with her," I yell. "Why are you even here? I'm not your employee anymore. I'm nothing to you."

"Listen to yourself. You're using this whole fucked-up situation to run again because that's what you do. You sabotage things before they even have a chance to be good. The only thing I'm guilty of is not telling you the truth about Kassius and my initial tabs on you. Once he befriended you, I felt that was his truth to tell."

"You're wasting your breath, Mr. Lair. I don't believe you. Why would a rich man like yourself waste his time on fucking maids? It's a sick fetish that satisfies your god complex. You fucking drink half million dollar champagne when some of us can't even afford to buy a camera or a house," I rant. "You even dress down and wear that stupid key that is worthless considering your millions. It was all an illusion. You appeal to our common ground of simplicity when really it's just one of your tricks to continue collecting us maids." I choke on my own tears. I'm winded from unleashing all that fury.

Even after several seconds of silence, I refuse to look up at him.

"You have it all figured out, I guess. And all on your own. Nothing else left for me to say. Just know that key that you deem worthless is my daily reminder of this very thing. Thank you for reiterating why it's necessary." His voice sound strangled. Different.

I want to look, but I can't. Is he crying? Can't be. "I will grant your wish, Brennan. I will see that you are paid for the entire duration of this cruise. I will have Atticus arrange for my private helicopter to take you back to Florida or wherever you want to go. We're scheduled to arrive at our next port in two days. He will arrange your departure for then."

CHAPTER 20

Brennan

The finality of his words guts me. There is a physical ache in my chest. Bile bubbles up, threatening to make me vomit. This hurts too badly, and I'm paralyzed to this spot. Somehow, I know I will never be the same again. I anticipated that things would eventually run its course, but not like this.

"Goodbye, Brennan. I wish you well." He turns to leave the way he came, and as soon as the door closes, I throw the only thing in my reach. My phone. My last connection to him. It shatters against my cabin door in splintering pieces. He can just deduct it from my check.

I don't know how long I lie on the floor before there is another knock on my door. All concept of time escapes me. Just like the last time, I don't answer. The sun is no longer filtering through the curtains I left open. That's my only hint that it's now nighttime. The sound of a key card being entered beeps again, and I intentionally peek up, incorrectly assuming it's Silas. *Wrong.* It's the other Lair—the cousin.

"Brennan?" Kassius whispers into the dark. Maybe if I don't answer, he will go away. No such luck. He flicks on the light, and my eyes work to adjust.

"Ah, hell, Bren!" He stomps toward me, and I can't cower away fast enough before he has me picked up and placed on my bed. I swat at him like a wild cat backed into a corner. He just lets me hit him, not once restraining my arms. He holds me by the waist and lets me exhaust my frustrations.

"I hate you," I cry. "I hate all you." Especially all the fucking tears I've shed today, but I don't give him the satisfaction of that info.

"Get it all out. Hit me. Do whatever you need to do. Then we will talk."

What fucking nerve! "I'm not talking to you,

jackass. I don't have anything to say to you or your traitor maid-collecting cousin," I curse.

His absence of the gay air fuels my anger. It's as if a complete stranger is in this room with me—or might as well be. I can't believe I could be so wrong about not only one but two people. I let my guard down. He encouraged me to give Silas a chance, for fuck's sake. Is this their thing? Tag team the stupid housekeepers.

I can no longer keep the bile down; it's no longer just an urge. I tear away from Kassius and run to the toilet with only seconds to spare. I end up dry heaving because my stomach is empty since I missed dinner.

Kassius comes in behind me, takes a washcloth from the towel rack, and wets it. I brace the porcelain, exhausted. I have no fight left in me to push him away as he pats my face with the cool towel.

"I'm still not talking to you," I manage to get out between heaves.

"Well, you can listen then because I'm not leaving until you hear everything I have to say. After that, if you still choose to hate me, I will respect that."

It's pointless to argue. I can see the conviction in his narrowed eyes. I will let him talk, and then I will kick him out. I have two days to determine what the hell I'm going to do with my life.

Kneeling here and dry heaving over the toilet

brings about Deja vu. Not too long ago, Silas was here while I was sick. Even with my head almost in the toilet, I can't erase the memory of the despair I heard in his voice as he left. I'm trying not to care, but I'm failing miserably. I only half believe all those nasty things I threw at him. I just wanted to hurt him with my words … give him a taste of what I was feeling. I didn't feel used when I was with him, but I'm not sure how much of what I felt was an illusion orchestrated by a master player.

When it is obvious that I have nothing to come up, Kassius wipes my face and helps me to my feet. I pull away from him, and he pulls back. He wants to help me to my room. Fine. I sit on my bed, and he sits on the empty one opposite of me.

"I'll start from the beginning," he announces when he is satisfied he has my attention.

"After our brief meeting before the guests arrived, Silas asked me to stay behind for a special task. He told me that he had hired a new housekeeper because Atticus asked for a favor for a friend. All his employees were investigated and well vetted before being hired, but he didn't have time to do that with you. The request from Atticus's friend was sudden, and the cruise was leaving before he could get proper intel on you. He is very protective of his business. I won't get into specifics, but there are people who would love to see him fail—to bring down his entities."

"I signed his NDA," I point out.

"That's nowhere near enough. Anyone can sign a piece of paper. The trick is to ensure that the person signing is reliable and trustworthy enough to adhere to what is being signed."

"So what does all this have to do with you? Why did you lie to me?"

"Someone from the aft leaked aspects of *The Playboy's Lair*. They didn't have access to our proprietary info, but it was enough for Silas to get wind of a copycat in the BDSM community. They tried to start their own cruise, similar to ours, but it tanked because their idea didn't hold the connections and prestige of ours. We could not decipher who the guilty person was, and our best guess was that it wasn't an individual effort. Four of us co-own *The Playboy's Lair*. As partners, we mutually decided to let go of the entire group of employees. That is why Silas needed seven volunteers from his remaining staff to work the aft—why he needed to have an initial eye on you. Someone got to one of his original staff members, who then potentially poisoned more employees to be a part of their plan to steal his ideas. He needed to be sure about you."

"So innocent people lost their jobs in the process?"

I told myself that I wouldn't speak, that I'd let him explain himself so he could leave, but now he's caught me off guard with what he's shared. I feel horrible for those people who didn't have a hand in betraying Silas, but it gives me insight into his reasons for having me investigated.

"Casualities of war, I'm afraid."

"That's so sad. One question. Why did you pretend to be my friend ... and gay?"

"I wasn't pretending with the friend part, Brennan. I only gave you a fake name because I had to. I've hosted experiences on this cruise. The volunteer employees who were brought over to the aft on our floor knew who I was. We had to keep my identity exclusive to those two, Ben and Jacob. Do you know how hard it was to avoid any staff who would recognize me?"

He comes over to sit on the bed next to me. "You were a breath of fresh air, Brennan. Although I had to create a persona, our interactions were real. You needed a girlfriend, not some macho guy trying to befriend you. I knew you would never let me in as myself so I gave you an alternate version you could relate to—a gay guy. The persona and his background I created was the only thing I faked. The way I feel about you is real. You're the sweetest, most genuine person I've met in a long time. I knew the minute Silas begin to fall for you.

When he found out about our friendship, he encouraged me to tell you, but we wanted to do it together. He needed to explain why I was originally put in your path. He wanted to talk to you about something very important first, and now I don't know if it will ever happen."

"What did he want to tell me?" My curiosity is piqued.

"That will have to come from him. Silas really is a good guy. He is very protective of his heart, careful not to let people in, but if you're fortunate enough to be allowed in, he loves hard."

"I said some very mean things when he came by earlier," I admit.

Now that the anger is wearing off, I'm filled with regret. I don't know if any of what those women said was true. All I have to go by is how special he made me feel.

"Trust me, I know. I've never seen my cousin look so distraught. You had the ability to wreck him, and you did just that. He wouldn't tell me what you said, but he told me that you'd be departing when we get to the Barbados port." Kassius untangles my fingers and lifts my chin. "Hear him out, Bren. Don't leave without giving him a chance to express himself. I'll let you be. I don't expect to mend things with you overnight, but I hope we can rebuild our friendship."

I don't reply. I can't give him an answer right now. Chance are, I will never see him again anyway. He leaves, and I'm left alone with my thoughts.

I need to return Silas's camera to him. This is my rationale for now heading to his room. I simply can't put it off. Just my luck, his level is open from the indoor pool area still. I climb the stairs quickly, blocking any logic that tells me not to do this. I'm mere steps from the fire pit when I see them sitting there. He's with Jasper. She looks relaxed with a glass of red wine in her hand and legs crossed on the sofa. Silas is sitting next to her. He sits up straighter when he sees me, but it's obvious I've interrupted whatever the hell they're discussing. It's definitely not arguing, like earlier. I stand there tongue-tied, embarrassed.

"Is there something I can help you with, Brennan?"

The absence of his terms of endearment for me doesn't go unnoticed. Received and noted. His blue eyes are cold. I don't know this Silas.

"Just wanted to bring back your camera. Thank you for loaning it to me. I'll let you two ..."

I don't even attempt to finish that sentence. My heart crumbles at the word "two" as the possibility of them rekindling their past becomes more than a likely scenario. I place the camera bag at my feet, where I stand, and run away as fast as my legs will carry me. Only I can't go back to my room. It's the place where he first cuddled with me, the place I started to have feelings for him. Now he's already back with her. I get the sickening feeling in my gut because it's always been her. We were the substitutes, just like she said.

I don't even know why I bothered. I pushed him away without listening to his side, but from the looks of his coziness with her, he is just fine. Maybe we did have a spark, but now we'll never know. I do believe things happen the way they're meant to. Realizing I can't avoid my room forever, I head there instead of walking around the yacht like a lost soul. I need to find a place to go, but I don't have a computer, and I smashed my phone. That was a really smart move on my part.

I shower, crawl into bed, and turn on some *I Love Lucy* reruns. Whoever said it was better to have loved and lost than to never have loved at all doesn't know what the fuck they're talking about. *Fuck love.* I have more important things to worry about like not ending up homeless. I will worry about my future tomorrow as I'm sure it will still be just as bleak. I fall asleep to the shenanigans of Lucy and Ethel.

SILAS

A *Playboy's Lair* NOVEL: PART TWO

Sneak Peek

PROLOGUE

Silas

WHEN DID I GET THIS FUCKING SOFT? MY reputation precedes me. *Arrogant. Cocky. Ruthless.* My competitors wish to imitate me, men wish they could be me, and women wish for the chance to fuck me. My reflection stares back at me, illuminated by the flames from the fire pit. I don't recognize this man. He is a shell of who I once was. The truth is, he's been missing since Brennan showed up on my deck. Unbeknownst to me, a void existed in my life. One that she filled so easily. She chipped away at the armor I erected—the armor that transitioned me from a boy with feelings to a man with goals. These goals drove me to the success that I have been able to acquire. Neither love nor emotions were ever part of that equation. That mentality has allowed me to dominate the sex industry and to be the most sought-after billionaire bachelor to date.

I let my guard down for the appeal of innocence and naïvety. Foolish to think those attributes weren't a threat. In hindsight, Brennan was the most danger-ous of them all. She slipped through my defenses, un-derestimated. She made me want something that has no place in my life. *Love.* I could honestly see myself building something with her. Then out of nowhere, Jasper appears back in my life. With her came all the dormant feelings that I thought were long gone. My present and my past collided, taunting me and expos-ing my one weakness.

I have to find a way to turn it off. This fucking key around my neck is my armor. *My truth.* I must repel anything and anyone who threatens its purpose. My mind has been compromised—my flesh weak. My heart needs to be at its strongest. I watch as Jasper leans back on the loveseat, unbothered by Brennan's intrusion moments ago. She sips on her glass of red wine with her legs crossed. I've tuned out what she's said over the past couple of minutes. Instead, my mind drifts back to the conversation with Brennan some hours ago. Well, her accusation since she did all the talking. Disdain dripped from her words, her intent … malicious. She wanted to hurt me. She used verbal assault to do what she always did … run. So quick to judge, no benefit of the doubt given. She was too eager to believe the worst about me, thus successfully removing my blinders.

I watched the hurt in her eyes when she found me sitting here with Jasper, no doubt assuming the worst and creating the fictional scenarios in her head that she is so good at. I ignored the sinking feeling in my stomach, the hero complex that wanted to reach out and comfort her. She was met with a façade, an acceptable version of myself. Gone is the emotional ridden Silas. I will maintain this veneer until it becomes my truth yet again. *Cold. Calculating. Impenetrable.*

"You haven't said much," Jasper says after she notices my lack of response. I honestly have no clue what the hell she has even said.

"Hmmm. What was that?"

"We're you even listening?" She uncrosses her legs and leans forward to see my face.

I take a sip of my Macallan. "Not really."

"What was the point of asking me to your room then? I thought you wanted to clear the air," she replies frustrated.

"You assumed wrong. I haven't decided how I want to proceed. I summoned you here to decipher your true motive for being here. Only you chose to use the time to take a walk down memory lane, all while ignoring the amount of deceit involved to sneak aboard."

"I already laid it all out earlier. I explained my reasoning for everything. There was no other choice for me. I had to do whatever it took to see you again," she professes. "I was just trying to help you remember a happier time between us."

"None of it changes the facts. You plotted and executed a lie to get on board. That doesn't foster trust. Instead, it reveals your capability; the lengths you will go to get what you want."

"But it was for you."

I finish the last of my scotch and stand. This visit is over. The warmness I regarded her with, gone. Her argument is invalid. While I might see her perspective, I'm finding it hard to justify her actions. I can't help but think that ulterior motives may be at play here. I need to choose my next move wisely. The nostalgia of seeing her again has worn off, allowing me to think a bit clearer.

"It's getting late. I don't have an answer for you to-night. Your story is being validated, so we'll talk again tomorrow. This is good night."

I don't know what she hopes will be the outcome of all this. I've had some time to think about my options. It seems I only have one clear choice. Step back from them both. I recognize my weakness, and I'm choosing to eradicate it. Nobody will possess power over me. *Fuck emotions.* I was better off before without them. And definitely no more fucking my employees. I'm going to keep my business and sex life separate.

Jasper stands and tips back her glass to finish her wine. "I was going to wait to tell you this because I didn't want you to think I was trying to influence your decision to let me stay. Only now, it doesn't seem like anytime will be a good time. So before I go, I must confess something."

She kicks off her stilettos and brings them to her chest. She looks away from me and fixates on the fire. She starts at the beginning, revealing the most import-ant piece of the puzzle that she kept from me earlier.

My fucking world as I know it shatters into a million pieces. In mere seconds, she has managed to unravel any plans I may have hoped to make. She was holding the ace of spade, and she just played that motherfucker. *Fuck me.* I'm rendered speechless as she walks away hugging those stupid stilettos to her chest. If her plan all this time was to come aboard and wreck my life, she has succeeded. Now what the hell am I going to do?

CHAPTER 1

Brennan

1 week later

TODAY IS MY OFF DAY. IT'S BEAUTIFUL SATURDAY morning, yet I'm held up in my cabin. I watch the guests get off the yacht here in St. Kitts. I quit a week ago, but Kassius convinced me to stay. It was the hardest decision I've ever had to face. Going back to the Neumanns wasn't an option. My only two choices were to stay or to leave and struggle to find somewhere to stay. I don't have a credit history or rental history—nothing to make anyone want to rent to me. The choice was painfully obvious. Kassius had promised to help me once we arrive back in Florida, so I just have to hold on until then.

Things between us aren't exactly as they were before, but I've agreed that we could start over. No lies this time around. He talked to Silas for me to reinstate my job. Luckily, I didn't have to tuck my tail between my legs and beg. My phone was replaced, and the little thing called the cloud saved the pics I had taken on the other one. For that I'm grateful. There are even a couple of pics that I snuck of him that I try not to look at. He's not thinking about me, and I'd do well to do the same. I was transferred from the aft to the job I was originally hired for. I haven't seen Silas since. His normally open retractable ceiling has been closed to the pool below.

I've swum laps every night this week at midnight, telling myself that I'm just getting back to my routine. Failing miserably to convince myself that I'm not hoping to run into him. I know that Jasper is still on this boat, so it doesn't take a rocket scientist to guess he's probably back with her. There was no landing of the helicopter when we docked in Barbados, and I'm sure it isn't coming now that we've docked again. Jasper is on this boat to stay. The sooner I accept that, the better off I'll be.

Yes, I said some hateful things. I ran. Then I chased him off with my hurtful words. This time he has given up the chase. He has the person he's supposed to be with, so I'm of no consequence, but my heart still aches for him. He didn't fight for me. For us. Did he ever want it to be an us? I hate that things ended the way they did, but I hate it even more that things are irreparable.

I didn't get off the boat in Barbados, so through the rotation, I'm able to get off now. What's the point, though? I'm numb, and no amount of picture taking is going to rectify that. I just want to order room service, binge on reality TV, and hide away in my cabin.

I flip through the channels, restlessly. Work. Eat. Swim. Sleep. Repeat. This has become my life. Luckily, I've had little contact with Tory. Atticus has taken over as my immediate boss. He's never mentioned any of the drama, and for that I'm grateful. I'm taking it a day at a time—trying to move on. Hopefully, things will get easier once I'm off this boat—away from the memory of him.

I'm startled by a knock on my door. I'm not expecting anyone. Hell, I'm still wearing my pajamas. I begrudgingly get up to answer.

"Um, you look like shit, buttercup," Kassius announces as he walks past me.

"Thanks. Nobody else has to see me, so whatever. Aren't you getting off the boat with everyone else?"

"Yes, and that's why I'm here. I've come to collect you."

"Collect me?"

"You've been a hermit long enough. You need some fresh air. You're getting off this boat with me." He walks over and plops himself on my unmade bed. He pulls the remote from under his ass, that he mistakenly sat on, and clicks off the television.

"Thanks for the offer, but—"

"Oh buttercup, I wasn't offering. This is an intervention. I won't take no for an answer," he responds, cutting me off. I stare at him blankly. "Don't just stand there. Go shower and wash your hair. We have a full day ahead of us."

He crosses his arms and put his feet up. I want to fight him on this, but maybe I do need some fresh air. "You're insufferable; you know that?"

"Yep. Now chop-chop. Do you need me to pick you out something to wear?"

"No!" I say a little to forcefully. What is it about the Lair men and their need to go through my things? The last thing I need is his judgment at my options. He is always so put together. "I mean I got it. I won't be long."

I quickly pull out a pair jean cutoffs that I cut at the knees with my nicest tank top. With my back blocking his view, I grab my undergarments from the drawer before heading off to get ready. I swear he is so bossy, just like his cousin.

It takes me about a half an hour to look presentable. Kassius is dressed in a designer labeled button-down short sleeve shirt and knee-length shorts. His muscular build fills them out well. We look totally opposite on the fashion scale, yet he doesn't seem to care. He jumps off the bed to help me with my top knot. I can't help but giggle.

"What's so funny?" He looks at me puzzled as he secures the elastic around my still damp hair.

"You. I miss thinking you were gay. You helping with my hair is just a reminder. I've never really had a girlfriend before, and I had already claimed you."

"Hey now. You can't unclaimed me. You're stuck with me. I'm still me—just your boyfriend now."

There is a pregnant pause between us. I know what he means. He's still my friend who is a boy, but the comment sounds different from when I say girlfriend. Kassius is undeniably sexy, so to know that he sees me from a straight man's eyes makes things a little awkward. Not that I think he's interested in me; it's just now it's just different than before.

"There. You're good," he says adjusting my top knot. I give him a megawatt smile. "Come on, crazy girl."

And just like that, the awkwardness melts away.

"Wait. You're missing one thing." He pulls off the shades resting on his head and puts them on my eyes. "There. Perfect."

"I'm pretty sure these cost more than my whole outfit," I protest. I try to remove them, but he taps my hands.

"Hush. They look better on you, and they complete your ensemble." He winks at me, and I'm glad I'm wearing the shades. It doesn't have the same effect as when Silas does it, but I'm not sure how it makes me feel is exactly friendly either.

"Ensemble? You're wearing an ensemble. I'm wearing shorts I made with flip-flops. I don't think my outfit would qualify as such."

I chuckle, and he pulls me into a bear hug. I inhale the scent of his cologne, and I'm almost tempted to hug him tighter. I don't, though. What the hell is wrong with me. He tousles my hair in a sisterly way, and I'm brought back to the present.

"What am I going to do with you, woman? Who

cares about the actual definition of ensemble? You look nice, and my sunglasses looks great on you. Enough said. Let's do this."

He heads to the door, leaving me no choice but to follow. I quickly grab my ChapStick, debit card, ID, and room key card before stuffing everything in my pockets. "Ready," I announce.

He looks as if he's going to say something, but then he just gives me another wink. He is going to have to stop that. I bet he has no idea he's doing it—kind of like a reflex. Still, it's confusing. It's sexy. It's hard not see him as an available hot guy when he does that. He's sweet to me, and he's gorgeous—bad combination. My heart is still broken from the other Lair cousin. I'll just have to be extra careful not to let rebound emotions get the best of me. Kassius and I are working to rebuild our friendship. *Friendship*. Nothing more.

Kassius and I get off the yacht just in time to see the man who plagues my every waking thought. And he is not alone. Jasper is with him. She's wearing shorts that barely cover her ass cheeks with an off the shoulder halter top. Even I have to admit she looks amazing. Her Hercules sandals come up to her knees. A black limo pulls up, and I watch as Silas places a hand at the small of her back to guide her to get in. Again, I'm thankful for the sunglasses. I fight the tears that threaten to fall. I finally look away rather than watch him get in with her. I don't want to watch them drive away.

Kassius grabs my hand and squeeze. No words are needed. He was witness to the same scene that just played out in front of me. It's one thing to know Silas had been with her, but it is another thing to see it. I don't even know how I can put one foot in front of the other at the moment, let alone spend the day with Kassius. I want to be alone. I want to be hurt in private—not in front of him.

"Where do you want to go first, buttercup?"

I look back toward the ship, but before the words can leave my mouth, my suggestion is shot down.

"Anywhere, but there. You're not going back to your room. Today, you'll enjoy yourself. Today is about you."

"That's a tall order," I say barely above a whisper—afraid the hurt will be evident in my voice.

"That's okay. Challenge accepted," he assures me.

ACKNOWLEDGEMENT

After spending countless hours of getting a story just right, it still has a way to go before it can come to fruition. I'm blessed and thankful for the amazing team that helped to make Silas better than I could have imagined. These key players are Ryan "Stacks" Harmon (cover model—Silas), Golden Czermak (FuriousFotog), Sommer Stein (Perfect Pear Creative Covers), Jenny Sims (Editing4Indies), and Stacey Ryan Blake (Champagne Formats). I'm thankful for their critical eyes, encouragement, creativity, and incredible talent. Then, there is my promo team. Kylie Dermott (Give Me Books), and Debra Presley (Buoni Amici Press) rocked at helping to get Silas out there and into the hands of many blogs. Big thanks go to all the blogs who participated in the cover reveal, release day blitz, and release boost. Next I have a special mention about a colleague, a fellow cardiac operating room nurse named Claire Pohlman. Sometimes ideas for a story, character dialogue, etc. comes from a source you least expect. Claire told me a wildly hilarious story one afternoon and the context found its way into my writing. The phrase, "smug little bitch", taken from her story evolved into Silas' nickname—Mr. Smug Hottie.

When inspiration strikes, you just run with it. Last, but certainly not least, I want to thank my personal assistants, Lauren Weber and Heather Coker, for keeping me organized, motivated, and sane at times. They listen to my ideas and visions when I need sound advice. I can always count on them to be honest with their feedback. Everyone mentioned played a vital role with the creation of Silas. Each contribution is recognized and appreciated.

ABOUT THE AUTHOR

S.R. Watson is a Texas native, who currently resides in Wisconsin. She grew up reading the Sweet Valley series (Twins, High, & University) among others. Although she wrote countless stories during high school, she never published any of them. She continued her education and became a registered nurse. After reading the Twilight series and 50 Shades Trilogy, she decided to pursue her passion for writing once again.

S.R. Watson published the first book in 2014. She is the bestselling author of the Forbidden Trilogy, The Object of His Desire, and the co-authored S.I.N. Trilogy with Shawn Dawson.

When S.R. Watson is not writing, or working as a CVOR nurse, she loves to read and binge watch her favorite shows (Scandal, How to Get Away with Murder, Elementary, etc.)

Made in the USA
Las Vegas, NV
02 January 2022

39936337R00162